COSMIC CHAOS

CM SHELTON

Illustrated by
Joley Cadence

Ashberry Lane

© 2015 C.M. Shelton
Ashberry Lane Publishing
P.O. Box 665, Gaston, OR 97119
www.ashberrylane.com
Printed in the USA

ISBN 978-1-941720-25-7

Library of Congress Control Number: 2015951808

Cover design by Miller Media Solutions
Illustrations by Joley Cadence
Edited by Rachel Lulich, Kristen Johnson, Andrea Cox, and
Tami Engle

FICTION / Middle Grade / Science Fiction

12-6-15

Sloane –

Hope you enjoy the
story!

much love,
Carolin Marie

This book is dedicated to my four
ultra-cosmic kids: Kylie, Joley,
Devon, and Cody.

If you were ever taken from me,
I would pursue you ...
even to the far reaches
of the moon.

PROLOGUE

Earth
2031 A.D.

"No!" Logan locked his arms around his mom's neck. "I *won't* go without you."

Dad pulled at Logan's waist. "There's no time for this."

His mother squeezed Logan tighter. "Just give me a second," she pleaded. She gently pulled his arms down, then wiped the volcanic ash off his face mask. "Look at me."

He squinted at her.

An intensity filled her eyes. "As soon as it's safe, I'll—"

A quake jolted the ground, and he stumbled.

Evacuation sirens blared.

As his dad flung him onto his broad shoulders, Logan's neck whiplashed.

"We have to go, *now!*" his dad shouted as they raced

1

toward the moon shuttle.

Over the chaos, his mom yelled, "I'll come get you, Logan. I *promise*!"

Chapter One
RED ZONE

2036 A.D.

"You can't make me," the new boy said.

Red lights flashed on the teacher's built-in belly screen as she hovered closer.

Logan's heart raced at warp speed. His fingers flew across the type pad in front of him. *Don't say another word or you'll get zapped!* He hit Send.

The message appeared on the boy's desk screen.

The new kid turned and sneered at Logan. "I'll do what I want."

A collective gasp came from the students.

Logan's pale hands shook.

A stasis beam shot out from the teacher's side, enveloping its target. "Code Red," she announced. "Noncompliant student."

Immobilized, the new kid floated into the air, unable to move or speak.

An electromagnetic energy beam shot down from

the ceiling, crackling like a downed power line. It encircled the new kid with purplish neon volts. An electric buzz filled the room, sparking the air.

All the students dove under their desks for cover.

The new kid shot upward as the beam lifted him into the ceiling's portal, fast as lightning. Then, he was gone.

As the energy beam shut down, a quiet hush overtook the room.

Hunkered down on the floor, Logan released his hold from the desk legs. Every muscle felt weighted down as he crawled into his chair. He looked out across the sterile room, crisscrossed with hundreds of desks.

The students, clad in their silver uniforms, crept along the stark-white floors back to their chairs as if waking from a nightmare.

At the front of the class, words flashed on the main digital screen.

CONFORM AND SUBMIT

The sound of fingers tapping on touch screens filled the room as students resumed their work. Bald heads lined the rows in perfect submission.

Logan looked up at the security cameras instead of focusing on the science diagram on his desk screen. His temples throbbed. He strained to suck in the frosty, thin air.

Two kids turned and stared as he breathed in short gasps.

Hup ... hup ... hup ... His clumsy hands reached for the emergency oxygen mask attached to the side of his desk, nearly knocking it to the floor. With the mask finally in hand, he mashed it to his face, desperately inhaling deep breaths of pure oxygen.

In, out. In, out.

His lungs relaxed.

The student next to him scratched at her ID chip implant. The shape of a twisted star, the implant spread across the back of her left hand, the points stretched to every knuckle. It looked like a metal tattoo branded into her flesh. The swollen skin around it screamed crimson red. *Painful.*

He closed his eyes for a moment, then opened them, bracing himself to get his science studies finished.

Forty minutes later a message rolled across his desk screen.

STAND FOR DISMISSAL

He stood, the thought of leaving this place strengthening his very bones, as it did every day. He kept his gaze on the floor, not looking at anyone.

The other students held up their left hands,

exposing their implants for scanning.

Blip, blip, blip. Like a checker at the grocery store, the teacher scanned each student, downloading the evening's homework.

When she reached Logan, there was no blip.

Just silence.

She stopped suddenly, belly screen flashing: *No identity chip implant.*

His neck flooded with heat.

The teacher's sleek, silver body reflected the glaring lights overhead. "PTD override," her silicon voice declared. "Medical exemption. Code nine-six-four." She stared down at him with pulsating yellow eyes, digital pupils snapping shots of his every move.

A Personal Tracking Device chip, loaded with hours of homework, ejected from her mouth.

The thought of homework sent negative particles spinning through Logan's stomach. His hands grew clammy as he reached for the chip.

The teacher moved on to the remaining students. *Blip, blip, blip.*

He clutched the oxygen mask with both hands, dragging in more air, two, three times, steadying himself against his desk.

A headache pressed into his skull.

Logan smacked the tank to get the last of the

oxygen, then dropped it onto his desk. The teacher would replace it by the next morning. With the exit rush over, he took slow, deliberate steps to the doors, careful not to make his headache worse.

The doors hissed open, and he stepped out of the classroom and onto the conveyor belt. Students pressed into him as they crowded out of class, riding along through the main hall. The noise level rivaled that of a rocket race with kids cheering for their favorite pilot.

The hammering in Logan's head steadily grew worse. He covered his ears, concentrating on getting out of this place. Fast.

"Hey, wait up," someone called.

A touch fell on Logan's slouching shoulders. He turned to face a boy about his age, but much taller.

"It's okay to talk out here, right?"

Logan nodded, then cringed at the throbbing. He strained his eyes to get a better look at this kid. Ears poked out of his head like hovercraft wings ready for flight. A silver earring dangled to his shoulder. A round, red tattoo on his neck indicated time spent at Juvi Hall on Venus. Logan had never seen this guy before.

"I'm Jet," the kid said over the noisy chaos. "Pretty dumb what Warner did today, huh?"

"Who's Warner?" Logan asked.

"He came over from Neptune with me last night."

Logan arched a weary eyebrow. "Humans haven't colonized Neptune yet."

Jet didn't seem to hear. His eyes shifted sideways before jutting his chin out. "Warner always was a troublemaker." A snorty laugh came from his pierced nose as he gave Logan a playful push. "You watch. He'll talk in class again tomorrow."

Logan stumbled backward. "I doubt it." He worked to steady himself. "Once he recovers from his nerves being zapped, he'll be drugged. And if that won't keep him compliant, they'll double the dosage each day until he's pretty much a zombie."

Jet's mouth dropped open. "Really. I guess they're pretty strict around here." His eyes wandered, examining the security guards. "I sit right behind you in class." His lips curled back as he looked Logan over. "What's up with all the weird breathing sounds you make?"

Logan flinched and looked away. "Well …" Embarrassment heated his face as he attempted to give an explanation. "I just—"

The conveyor belt came to an abrupt end and Jet leaped off. "See ya tomorrow!"

Logan blinked for a moment. "Sure." He stepped

off as Hovercraft Ears rushed away to his next destination. At least Logan didn't have to explain. He pressed his lips together, then headed toward the docking station.

His pod hovered in the disabled zone. A drab coating of gray moon dust covered the rusted yellow paint.

Climbing in, he lifted his face for iris recognition.

"Good afternoon, Logan," the navigational unit stated.

"Take me to Troy's house."

The door clamped shut.

The monotone female voice sounded again. "Destination, home."

"What?" Logan shouted. He immediately regretted yelling. *The pod is supposed to take me to Troy's house.* Logan eased into the hard seat to cradle his aching head.

The pod released from its dock, creating a rattling and hissing sound.

A vise seemed to tighten on his skull. He stared out the window, waiting for the soothing motion of gliding through space to relax him. The pod maneuvered past the massive security gates, leaving the school fortress behind, and slipped into commuter traffic in a tunnel headed straight for the Luna Biodome. *The wrong direction.*

He sat forward, pressing buttons to change the GPS coding. He didn't like what he found. "Aw, come on, this can't be."

His headache began to lift.

"Dad," he called out. His strained voice sounded how he felt—small and miserable.

A screen dropped down in front of the window.

PLEASE HOLD

All the air in Logan's lungs escaped like gas from a deflating balloon. He grabbed an emergency oxygen mask and pressed it over his mouth and nose. He sucked in deep, desperate breaths. In, out. In, out.

His dad's face appeared on the 3-D projection screen. "Make it quick, Logan, I'm in the middle of a meeting." His authoritative voice filled the cockpit.

Logan pulled the mask down, just enough to talk. "You promised I could go to Troy's house after school today for Air Rocket rides," his voice quavered, "but the pod won't take me there. You programmed it to take me home."

His dad pointed a finger at him. "I received a notice this morning from your teacher." Accusation weighed heavily in his voice. "She said your PTD chip was returned empty."

Logan shrank back, gripping the seat. "It's not my fault." He glared down at the floor. *And you know it.*

COSMIC CHAOS

"Now, Logan." His dad heaved a deep sigh. "I understand Maggie's been having issues lately, but that doesn't mean you can't do your homework."

Logan's head popped up. "But—"

His dad held up a hand to silence him. "We'll discuss this later. I have to go."

The screen clicked off.

Hot flames scorched Logan's gut. *If Maggie messes up again, I'll end up just like that new kid, Warner. Fried to a crisp.*

Chapter Two
BLACK HOLE

Logan stared out the window as his pod sputtered alongside commuter traffic. He didn't want to think about school. *Wouldn't* think about school.

Sleek, high-powered pods swerved dangerously close, cutting him off as the tunnel opened up to the Luna Biodome.

The city of Luna spread before him, its massive skyscrapers dominating the horizon. Their yellow lights were barely visible through the gray haze of fine moon dust, known as mog. It lingered in the air and coated everything. Air-purifying towers, resembling stacks of gray pancakes, stood every thousand feet inside the perimeter of the dome, attempting to keep the air clean. Just looking at the hazy air made Logan's lungs tighten, sending him into a coughing fit.

Massive horizontal tubes lined the ground, shooting cargo from underground factories to corporate and residential destinations. In the air, pods, ships, and hovercrafts flowed at a constant frenzy. With no one but autopilots to provide air traffic control, accidents were common. But Logan had been lucky so far, with only a few rear-enders and a couple of mild sideswipes during his five years on the moon.

The blinking blue lights of a satellite seemed way too near to the Luna Biodome as it floated in space. If it collided with the dome overhead, it could easily crack the AcryFab. That dome was the only thing keeping the sun from scorching everything. He once heard his dad joking about the moon wearing expensive sunglasses. But the system worked too well, keeping the temperatures in both of the main domes much too cold.

He shivered. If only his dad would buy him the double thermal uniforms, like most of the students had.

Traffic slowed as he commuted past the massive oxygen tubes and fans, only half of them active. On one tube, a repair team hung precariously from thick cords, wearing safety harnesses.

His pod turned, sputtered, then backfired.

Logan slunk down in his seat to avoid the stares of other commuters. He smacked his fist against the dashboard. "C'mon, work right!"

The pod broke away from traffic and headed straight for the cluster of dingy apartments on the left. "Finally," he mumbled. "As soon as Maggie is working

13

right, I'm calling Troy."

"Please repeat request," the navigational unit stated.

He rolled his eyes to the ceiling, wishing they had decimating laser powers.

At floor 58, the ninth garage door to the right slid open. The pod clicked as it docked into its home station.

Maggie rolled out to meet him. As the pod door slid open, her words crackled, "To, to, to … to the viral chamber."

"I know." Logan didn't even look at her. "You don't have to tell me every day." He walked past her and into his home, nothing but chilly air greeting him. He stepped into the viral chamber.

The white laser beamed over his body from top to bottom.

Sᴢᴢᴢᴢᴢ …

Faint sizzling sounds indicated the death of each germ.

"Puh-puh-puh …" Maggie attempted to say something.

Logan walked out. He knew the drill. He pulled the PTD chip from his pocket and inserted it into Maggie's metal side.

"You have a lot of homework tonight," she said clearly. "Why so mu-mu—" Garbled sounds jumped

14

through the air from her mouth.

Logan's body went rigid as he kept himself from whacking her robot face. "If you hadn't deleted all the work I did last night, I wouldn't have so much tonight."

A beep sounded at the other end of the room.

Logan spun around.

The word *INCOMING* flashed across the hologram screen.

Mom? Please be Mom. He sat down on the cold, white floor. "Receive."

A holographic image appeared in front of him.

"Hey, Logan."

"Hey, Troy." Logan smiled, even though his stomach dropped with disappointment.

Troy jumped around with the energy of a two-year-old. "Where are you? It's almost time for the Air Rocket rides."

Logan sighed. *How do I explain this to Troy?*

Troy didn't wait for a response. "Get over here soon. We're having a mega eclipse party tonight. My mom is lighting a bunch of candles and—"

"Co-co-code four-seven-five states burning candles is illegal." Maggie rolled closer.

Logan covered his forehead with the palm of his hand. If only he could disappear.

"You haven't replaced that old bucket yet?" Troy asked.

"Working on it." Logan shot an icy photon stare at Maggie.

"Well, anyway, my dad is importing *spring water* from Earth." Troy said the words as though he spoke of something holy. "You need to be here."

"I'll be there. No way am I missing it." Logan lowered his chin and raised an eyebrow. "What's the difference, anyway? Earth water is Earth water, right?"

Troy shrugged. "I dunno. My dad says spring water is the best there is." He leaned in, lowering his voice. "He also said to keep it quiet, so don't tell anyone."

"What time?"

Troy disappeared as the holographic image shut down.

Logan looked up. "Maggie! Turn it back on. We were in the middle of a conversation."

Only two of her words came out clear: "homework" and "now."

"Aw, come on." He stood with slow movements as the pressure returned to his head.

Maggie rolled across the floor, her bulky tracks *clack-clacking* with each turn.

"Sounds like you have a broken track." He pulled a toolbox away from the wall and dug through the

16

contents, searching for the right part. "Found it. Come over here."

Maggie rolled to him, bumping into the wall and nearly tipping. Her model identification, printed in red on the back of her right shoulder, was terribly faded.

MAGGI LX New Technology for a New Way of Living

He grunted. Her "new technology" had been outdated six months after going into production. "What's happening on Earth today?" He squatted down and carefully removed the broken piece. "Any news?"

"Today's data collected," she said in her monotone voice.

"Well, let's hear it, then."

A clutter of sounds burst forth from Maggie, as

17

though she was attempting to find a radio station. Finally, she projected the voice of the newscaster. "The One World Galaxy Foundation announced this morning that all attempts at Earth's restoration have come to a halt. They are requesting-ing-ing ..."

"Come on, Maggie." He thunked her box-shaped body with the handle of his screw driver.

"... until funds can be raised to continue the project-ect-ect-ect."

Logan sighed. "I'll never see Mom at this rate." He snapped the new track into place.

"Repeat," Maggie said. Her empty, black eyes looked straight ahead.

"Nothing." He tossed the broken track into his toolbox. "All right, give it a whirl, and let's see if it's any better."

Maggie rolled smoothly across the floor ... except for the loose wires dangling dangerously close to her tracks.

"Come back over here. That rusty hinge needs to be replaced so those wires won't keep falling out."

One of them sparked at his touch.

"Ouch!"

"Homework is priority."

Logan dropped the screwdriver into the toolbox drawer. He slammed it shut. "All right. Let's get it over with. What am I supposed to work on today?"

"Processing-ing ..."

"Don't start that again." Logan smacked Maggie's side with his open hand.

"Processing-ing-ing-ing ..."

Logan grabbed a wrench and banged Maggie until her sides dented.

"PTD chip data deleted."

"What? No! I can't believe you did this again!"

"—ing-ing-ing ..."

His head pounded. He needed air. He grabbed the emergency oxygen kit from the table and placed the mask over his face. He bent over, gulping the air in deep breaths. *Just relax ... everything is going to be fine.*

Until the teacher finds out my homework isn't done. Two days in a row.

His eyes flew open, and he sucked in another gulp of air as his hands shook.

Suddenly, a thought poured into his mind, gliding in smoother than the Milky Way. *Maybe I can convince Dad to let me go to Troy's house to use HIS robot. Then I'll get my homework done* and *get to go to the party.*

Logan yanked off the mask. He went to the hologram projector and called his father.

"She did it again." Logan stared intently at his dad's holographic image. "My PTD chip is deleted. Again!

19

Do you know how much trouble I'm going to be in at school?" Logan pressed his fingers into his temples. "She needs to be replaced." He didn't sound as confident as he wanted to.

"Now, son, I'm not entirely convinced the problem is Maggie." His dad turned, leaning toward the whispering of a coworker. Then he swiveled back to Logan. "I've got to get going. Testing starts in five minutes."

"What do you mean?" Logan pleaded with his eyes.

"The new oxygen system they've put me in charge of—"

"No, I'm talking about what you said about Maggie. You said you weren't convinced the problem is her. What do you mean by that?"

His dad shook his head and sat back. "You might be using her as an excuse for not getting your homework done."

"What?" Logan's neck stiffened. "I wouldn't do that."

"I have to get going, son. The boss is on his way over—"

"But can't we just buy the Nanny Express Five Thousand? Troy has one. They're *ultra-cosmic*."

"We can't afford that." His dad turned and held a hand up to someone, motioning for the person to wait.

COSMIC CHAOS

"But, Dad, you just got a promotion. And you *know* Mom would approve."

His dad leaned in and spoke quietly, "I'm setting money aside for us. For"—he looked over his shoulder—"you know … what we talked about. It'll take every cent we've got." His eye twitched. "Don't tell anyone."

Logan willed himself to speak rationally. "All right. Then can I at least go to Troy's house and do my homework there? He says I can use his robot anytime." His words spilled out fast, before his dad could end the conversation. "And he's having an epic party tonight. I promise I'll get all my homework done before the party starts."

"That's fine. Just make sure your homework gets done *before* you go."

"But—"

"I gotta run."

The holographic image clicked off.

Logan's stomach plunged into a black hole. *Dad doesn't even care.*

Chapter Three
FIRE

Logan kicked the chair over. He grabbed the wrench and lifted it high to smash the hologram projector.

Sharp pain pierced his chest.

"Aah!" The wrench clattered to the floor as Logan dropped to his knees and sagged heavily against the fallen chair. His fingers reached for the oxygen mask. Mashing it into his face, he gulped the air in.

In, out. In, out.

He relaxed as the pain subsided, and his gaze lingered on the aquarium on the small dining table nearby.

The goldfish swam in circles as if it didn't have a care in the galaxy.

Hey, little Doppler. And they said you wouldn't survive.

As if the fish could hear his thoughts.

Bright green pebbles covered the bottom of the tank, an odd contrast to the colorless apartment. Large bubbles spluttered to the top, the oxygen coming from Logan's second emergency supply tank.

COSMIC CHAOS

As his lungs relaxed, he sprinkled fish food into the aquarium. He tapped the food container against the side of the glass, attempting to shake out the last bits. He removed the mask from his face. "I hope Mom sends you more food soon, Doppler. Otherwise, I'll have to find you something else to eat."

Last time I heard from Mom …

"I hope you like it." His mom's holographic image had stood in front of him. "I had to pull some strings to …"

Her image and voice faded in and out for a moment.

"Thanks, Mom." Maybe the connection was better on her end.

She laughed, her silken, brown hair falling across her shoulder. "But you haven't even seen what it is. Open it."

He snapped open the box, delivered just that morning, and lifted the lid. Inside was an aquarium, various supplies, and a clear plastic bag. It held water. Real, fresh water.

Something orange moved around inside it.

A fish! He'd seen vertebrates before in an interactive program, but never in real life.

"Do you like it?" His mom's face shone.

The fish zipped around in the little bag.

"It's ultra-cosmic."

She laughed, a sound like music. He wished he could hear her laughter more often. Then her voice grew heavy. "I love you, Logan. I want you to always …" Her voice had slipped away.

Obnoxious buzzing had filled the line.

"Can-uuutttt …" Maggie's voice cut into his memory.

His head jerked up. He turned toward Maggie and glared at her. "Yeah, I know," he spit. "I have to fix you myself, since Dad won't buy a replacement." He pulled out the toolbox again and yanked on her dangling wires. "It's not like I'll be going anywhere tonight, anyway."

Logan woke the next morning to the sounds of sizzling. "Ugh. Maggie's circuits must be fried."

Smoke hovered against the ceiling.

He sprinted out of bed.

Maggie stood in the kitchen. "Co-co-co … code three-six-seven states fires are illegal."

A small fire blazed on the countertop in front of her.

Logan froze. *Fire?*

The oxygen vents kicked on.

Adrenaline surged through him faster than electron

24

volts as the flames doubled in size.

He shouted at the hologram projector. "Dad!"

A voice responded. "Hold, please."

Logan swung back, helplessly staring at the blazing flames.

They crept from the counter onto Maggie's apron.

She was saying something else now, but he couldn't make out the words.

"What is it, son?"

Logan spun around. His voice screeched, "Dad! There's a fire. What do I do?"

His dad appeared stunned. "Uhhh ..."

Logan coughed as the smoke thickened.

His dad jolted to his senses. "I'll turn off the main oxygen supply from here. You need to smother the fire with a blanket, or ... or water, or *something*."

Logan covered his mouth, lungs burning as he turned toward the kitchen.

The aquarium full of water.

That will do it. But I have to get Doppler out. He cupped his hand to fish out his pet, peering through the smoky air.

His hand came out empty.

C'mon, where are you?

The flames grew bigger.

Logan couldn't wait any longer. He dumped the

water over Maggie and the countertop.

Black smoke rose like an atomic bomb from the charred remains.

Logan bent over coughing, hacking and gasping for air as he turned toward the hologram.

"Son, are you okay?"

Logan coughed again.

"I'm calling the paramedics. Hang on!"

Logan stumbled to the table and grabbed his emergency oxygen. He shoved the mask to his mouth and breathed deeply, trying not to cough. Was the fire out?

Although singed and smoking, Maggie still spoke. "Breakfast is ready. Breakfast is ready."

Breakfast? Had she been trying to cook something?

His gaze wandered over the blackened kitchen counter. She had definitely made a fire, but ... *What would she cook?*

Maggie held a pan.

Something small lay in it.

Logan stepped closer. His heart grew heavier than an orbiting satellite.

Doppler.

COSMIC CHAOS

Chapter Four
SPINNING VORTEX

"How did you get hold of so much water to put out the fire?" one of the paramedics asked. He wore the same thermal uniform as everyone else, but it was blue instead of silver. He scanned Logan's chest, then read the data on his handheld medical device.

"My aquarium." Logan's lungs still burned and he coughed often. But even worse than not being able to breathe was the truth that Doppler was gone.

"What?" Another paramedic blew out a low whistle. "I didn't know those still existed. That must have cost you a fortune to fill it."

"Well, I doubt you'll be filling it again anytime soon," the first paramedic said. "Have you heard the news?"

Logan shook his head. He couldn't exactly get the latest news from Maggie in her current condition.

"All water transportation is being halted." A frown joined the paramedic's words. "Too many drivers have been caught smuggling humans to Earth."

COSMIC CHAOS

I wonder if Dad heard about that. Logan's chest tightened even more. *It means we won't be able to …* His thoughts turned into a spinning vortex and tears threatened to surface. He turned his face away from the men.

The second paramedic shook his head. "It's back to drinking synthetic water for a while." He returned his instruments to their case. "Well, Logan, looks like you'll be just fine. Stay home today, get some rest, and you can return to school tomorrow."

A small robot, with a bright-red medical shell, hovered near them. "Digi-document is ready for transfer."

One of the paramedics took hold of Logan's hand and lifted it for scanning. Then stopped. His eyebrows came down as his lips scrunched up. "Where's your chip implant?"

Logan pulled his arm away. "I don't have one. I have chronic altitude sickness and a life-threatening allergy to moon dust. The doctor said an implant is too risky in my condition."

"Hmm, must make life a lot harder on you. Poor kid." He patted him on the shoulder, then turned to the robot. "Just transfer the information to a PTD chip. He can take it to school with him tomorrow. In the meantime, I'll submit a medical alert to your teacher with notification of today's absence."

A beep sounded at the other end of the room.

Logan turned to look at the screen.

INCOMING

He let out a hard cough, then sucked more air from the emergency mask. "Receive." His words sounded raspy.

His dad's holographic image appeared, shoulders sagging and his eyes appearing lifeless. "Logan. You okay?"

Logan nodded, waved to the paramedics as they left, then turned his attention back to his father.

"Have you heard the news?" His dad's words were barely audible. "About the smugglers being caught?"

Logan couldn't answer. His throat felt too tight.

"Just two more weeks." His dad let out a low groan. "That's all I needed. We would have been free from this place and joined her there."

Logan stared at his dad's agonized face while sucking in more air from the emergency mask.

"I've spent the last hour trying to cover my tracks so they wouldn't know we were on the list to be smuggled next." His voice grew frantic. "I just haven't figured out what to do with all the money I set aside. If they investigate me, I can't have the perfect amount just sitting there in my account." His jaw tightened. "If they suspect me, I'll be on the next shuttle to the Venus prison." His dad gave a sad laugh. "And then what would your mother say, huh?"

Logan stared at the floor. *I'll never see her again.*

"Breakfast is r-r-r-ready."

Logan jerked his head up and stared at Maggie. An idea flew into his mind, faster than the speed of light. "Use the money to get me the Nanny Express Five Thousand."

His dad blinked a few times. "Well, I suppose if Maggie is starting fires, she *does* need to be replaced." He nodded his head and sat a little straighter. "Last thing I need is to get fined for illegal fires. I'll get one ordered and delivered today."

The hologram clicked off.

Logan sank onto a chair. *Did he really just say that?*

Chapter Five
NEWLY IMPROVED

Two hours later, Logan stared at the huge container just delivered at his sky apartment. Bold, red letters covered the top half:

NE5K

Below that, smaller words.

Nanny Express Five Thousand is a state-of-the-art machine designed to care for your home and children better than any human. Newly improved version.

He pressed the yellow button and stepped back.

The door opened.

But his new machine didn't hover out.

He peeked in the door and gasped.

It wasn't a robot; it was a ... *woman.*

"Hello," she said, smiling, revealing teeth as white as starlight. Her sharp, blue eyes scanned the room, then settled on Logan.

He stared at her skin. It looked so soft. So *real.*

His friends' Nanny Express Five Thousands didn't look like this. She was even bald, just like everyone else.

COSMIC CHAOS

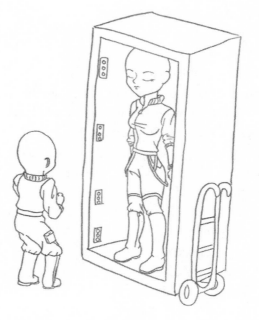

There must be some mistake. "Are ...?" He hesitated. What a dumb question to ask, but ... "Are you human?"

Her gentle laugh filled the emptiness of the room. "Do I look human?" She touched his arm. "I'd like to know more about you. May I scan you?"

"I ... don't have a chip implant."

"PTD chip?"

Logan pulled the chip from his pocket. Where was

he supposed to insert it? He didn't see any chip readers on her. *Maybe she IS human.*

A red laser beam shot from her eyes, scanning the chip he held.

Logan stumbled back.

"Hello, Logan," she said, voice warm as sun rays. "Now that I know all about you, we can begin."

Logan frowned. "Begin what?"

Her silver, lightweight moon boots, the same as his, tapped across the floor to the kitchen. She stopped where the charred blackness began.

"For you, it's time to begin your homework. And for me, it's time to clean up this mess." She pointed to the burned remains of Maggie.

"Wait. I want to keep her for replacement parts."

A perfectly manicured eyebrow rose. "Replacement parts for *me*?" A challenging smirk curled up one side of her mouth.

Well, yes. But for some reason he hesitated to say so. Maybe it would hurt her feelings. *Does she have feelings?* Who knew what new robots were capable of? "For, um, my friends' robots. I like to fix things."

She nodded her head slowly, still watching him with penetrating eyes. Then, with a quickness he wasn't expecting, she picked up Maggie as though she weighed nothing. The new robot carried her to Logan's room

34

and left her leaning against the wall. "There. Now you need to begin your homework."

Logan sighed. "I can't. Maggie deleted everything." His insides twisted tighter than a spiral galaxy.

"No problem." She lifted a shoulder. "I'll download the information from your school's database."

"You can do that?"

"I'm not supposed to." She winked.

"Ultra-cosmic!" Logan's shoulders relaxed as his assignments appeared before him.

The words hovered in the air, projected from her eyes.

He read the assignment out loud. "Write a five-hundred-word essay on the evolutionary process of Earth as it began millions of years ago. Include how Darwin's research and findings have impacted our understanding of life." Logan grunted. "A five-hundred-word essay? This must be yesterday's homework. I still have to re-do the day before too."

Nanny Express put a hand on his arm. "Allow me to help." She removed a bracelet from her wrist and snapped it around his.

Logan grinned. "Is this …?"

"Yes. It's a wrist remote for my interactive program. You simply—"

"I already know! I've used this program with

Crater's and Troy's robot-nannies."

"Let's begin, then. Every time you speak, I will record your input and automatically construct your essay."

"*Luminous.*" He said the word as if savoring a sweet moment.

The wrist remote flashed red.

The apartment went black, then transformed into the Galapagos Islands. The sunshine warmed his skin, mixing with a cool breeze that carried an unrecognizable scent.

He breathed in deeply.

Sparkling, turquoise waves reached out to touch his feet, then retreated. Wet sand sucked at his moon boots.

Everything—the sounds, the smells, the sensations—seemed so real. "This is *way* better than anything Troy's robot can do." He breathed in deep again.

Had his Nanny Express Five Thousand turned up the oxygen in the apartment?

He felt good. *Really* good.

A beep sounded from his wrist remote.

He glanced at the small screen.

YEAR: 1835

In front of him lay a vast sea and a wooden ship in

the distance. Painted on the ship's side was the barely legible word *Beagle*.

Deep-throated barking sounds came from behind Logan.

He turned and examined the island.

Brown, whiskered sea lions perched on black rocks.

"Young man," someone yelled.

Logan turned even more.

An elderly man waved his arms. He held papers in one hand and some sort of writing instrument in the other. "Get away from there, you idiot!" the old man hollered.

Where exactly was he supposed to go, then?

A sea lion barked and charged. Fast.

"You'd better run or you're gonna get bit!"

Logan chuckled. No one got hurt in an interactive program. *But then, none of the interactive programs I've been in seemed this real.* Logan took off running, just as the creature lunged at him.

Jaws snapped at his backside.

"Ahhhhh!"

Chapter Six
DISCIPLINE

Logan pushed himself to run faster.

Such freedom within the confines of a program was unheard of.

How long before I hit the wall of my apartment? He put a hand out to brace for impact, but nothing stopped him.

His lungs burned with exertion, and he looked over his shoulder.

The sea lion had stopped several yards away.

Keeping his hands out, Logan slowed to a stop, chest heaving. *I just ran, and I'm okay.*

"What's the matter with you, boy?" The stocky old man glared at him with haunting, dark eyes. A scraggly, white beard dangled from his blunt chin. "Didn't anyone ever tell you to stay away from a sea lion harem?" He spit tobacco juice through his teeth into the sand. "That bull nearly snapped your leg off."

Logan rolled his eyes. "Whatever." The warmth of the sun on his skin began to tingle. He looked up and squinted at the fireball in the sky. *The brightness in this program could bleach a person. Way overdone.*

But he couldn't leave yet, since he'd said nothing at all for his essay compilation.

He spoke into his wrist remote. "Galapagos Islands, 1835. This is where Charles Darwin discovered evolution." He blinked. "Or something like that. Maybe he saw evolution happening. Or ... oh, I don't remember. I'll ask." He spun around.

Grumpy Man was gone.

Logan scanned the grassy plains, then searched the beach.

The sea lions still lay there. Far ahead, the man walked away with determined steps.

What's up with that? If he's not around to answer questions, how am I supposed to do my essay?

A paper fell from the man's hand, drifting in the breeze until it caught on spindly grasses.

Bingo. I bet the answers are on that sheet. Awesome new program with awesome new challenges. Logan stepped forward. *Why not try running again?*

The air filled his lungs with sunny energy. The pumping of his legs, the swiftness of feet ... ultra-cosmic.

When he reached the paper, he lifted it, ready to read out loud for Nanny Express to compile.

Drawings and notes in scratchy handwriting

completely filled the page.

Huh? I can't read this.

At the bottom, a signature. *C. Darwin.*

Logan looked up. *So that's who Grumpy Man is!*

It didn't take long to spot the man, squatting over a dancing fire. His back was toward Logan, his once-white shirt half untucked. The heel of his leather boots pressed against the backside of his tan breeches.

Logan approached the campsite. A familiar burnt smell reached his nose.

Charles held a pointed stick over the flames, roasting something.

A fish.

A small, golden fish.

Doppler? Grief shackled his heart and buckled his knees. Hot tears flooded his eyes. His little orange friend, Doppler, was gone. The one living connection he had with his mom. Blackened and dead ... just like his soul.

Why would Nanny have allowed this to be in the program?

A deep ache pressed against his chest and wouldn't let go. It wasn't fair. Life wasn't fair. He kicked the log next to him as he cursed Nanny and pushed the End button on his wrist remote.

The islands disappeared.

COSMIC CHAOS

"Logan." A firm tone grounded Nanny's words as she appeared in front of him. "You haven't completed your homework. Let's begin the program again."

"No." Logan threw the wrist remote to the floor. "You did that on purpose, didn't you?" He shouted the words. As the breath left his mouth, his lungs deflated. He gasped for air.

Nanny swiftly retrieved Logan's mask and placed it over his mouth. "It's okay. Breathe deep." She rubbed his head as if he were a sleepy toddler.

He jerked away and pulled the mask down. "No way am I keeping you. I—" He gulped in more air from the mask, then pulled it down again. "I can't believe you did that to me." His voice shook. "You—"

It took too much effort to talk.

He stalked to his bedroom. *Idiot robot.* He threw himself onto the bed and pulled synthetic-fiber blankets to his chin.

Nausea crept through his belly like dark matter.

I wish Mom were here. He rolled over on his side and looked at the card on the nightstand.

Watercolor bunnies hopped across the front, carrying basketfuls of eggs.

He lifted the card and opened it.

Inside, the words *Happy Easter* were scribbled out. Written to the side: *Happy Birthday, Logan. Love, Mom.*

Even though the hologram connection was bad and kept cutting out, she'd made sure he understood. "My boss allowed me to leave the science center," she'd said, as though sharing a secret. "I went back to our old apartment. I knew I had a box of cards lying around somewhere, but couldn't find it. I didn't have time to search. Couldn't risk it." She gave a nervous laugh. "So I grabbed the first card I came across." She wrinkled her turned-up nose and her smile touched her warm, chestnut eyes.

Dad told Logan once he looked just like his mom.

Logan held one of the few organic things on the moon. If anyone found out, the card could be stolen or confiscated. He'd been lucky with Doppler ... until Maggie fried him.

I can't risk anything happening to this. He tucked the card into his toolbox drawer, hiding it from the all-seeing eyes of the moon.

"Logan, I don't have time for this." His dad rubbed the bridge of his nose with his thumb. "You've been begging me for the Nanny Express Five Thousand for over a year. Now that you have one, you don't want it?"

"You don't understand, Dad. She said she'd help me

with my homework, but she did a mean thing."

"A mean thing?" His dad sat forward. "You mean she disciplined you?" His face relaxed into a knowing smile, and he chuckled. "I've heard a lot of feedback about that with the Nanny Express. Kids these days don't like being disciplined." He thrust a finger at him. "Deal with it."

"No, that's not—"

"I said to deal with it," his father ordered, the smile gone. "End of discussion."

The hologram clicked off.

Without my homework done, I'm gonna be so dead.

Chapter Seven
GET IT RIGHT

"Logan, you don't have much time left to complete your homework."

He glared at the Nanny Express. "Like I'm going to let you do that to me again."

"I don't know what you mean." Her full lips pouted. "You haven't told me what happened." She walked her fingers up his arm and tickled his neck.

He grabbed her hand and flung it off. Spinning, he faced the kitchen.

Brand new panels covered the kitchen walls. Cabinets gleamed with a fresh coat of paint. The entire countertop had been removed and replaced with a sleeker, shinier surface.

"What did you do?"

"While you were brooding in your room, I removed all the burnt materials and replaced them. Much better, isn't it?"

"Where did the new materials come from?"

"I opened a credit line with Quasar Building

Company."

"Dad won't be able to pay for that."

"I will make the necessary adjustments to the household budget."

I'd better warn Dad. Maybe he can block her access to our account.

"Logan, whatever transpired in the interactive program earlier, I apologize." Her bald head reflected the overhead lights as her chin tilted. "Can we start over?"

Dad won't replace her. And I have to get my homework finished, unless I want to get zapped in school tomorrow. "All right. Fine." He took the wrist remote and snapped it on. "No islands this time. Just take me to Earth's origin, millions of years ago." He narrowed his eyes at her. "That should be safe enough, since fish hadn't evolved yet."

The wrist remote flashed red as the room went black.

A rumbling sound filled his ears.

A space shuttle? No. Maybe thunder.

Dark, towering clouds appeared. They flew by in the sky, moving swiftly with the wind.

Logan sucked the oxygen in. *More fabulous air. Must be a special feature with the newly improved Nanny.*

Maple trees framed the backside of a cream-colored

two-story house. A black machine sat in the grass, every blade behind it cut low.

A sliding glass door opened, and a girl stepped out. "Not yet!" she yelled into the house. "I have to finish mowing before it rains." She saw Logan and froze. Her eyes went wide as solar flares and she stepped back. "What are you doing here?"

He didn't have time to answer her questions. He needed *his* questions answered. *This obviously isn't millions of years ago.* "Stupid robot. She must be defective." He looked at the screen on his wrist remote.

YEAR: 2015

"Who are you?" Suspicion drove boldness into her voice.

He ignored the girl and fiddled with the wrist remote. *There must be a way to change the date manually.*

The buttons refused to cooperate.

"What's wrong?"

He could see her coming closer out of his peripheral vision. *Just what I need. More questions.* "Nanny Express," he said to his remote, "delete the character in front of me."

The girl gave a hard laugh. "What's that supposed to mean?"

She stood close now. Too close. He turned away from her. *Definitely a faulty robot if Nanny can't even delete a*

46

character.

"Oh, come on. Tell me," the girl persisted.

Logan rolled his eyes and shook his head, then turned and stared hard at her. "It's not like you're real."

She huffed. "What's that supposed to mean?" She was about the same age as him, with feathery, brown lashes and hazel eyes. She wore her silky, blonde hair in a long ponytail that swung back and forth with every move of her head, seeming to have a life of its own. An eyebrow rose with a sassy challenge.

He barked orders into the wrist remote loud enough to echo through the neighborhood. "I said a million years, Nanny. Get it right!"

Smirking, Ponytail Girl shifted her weight to the other leg.

Warmth rose into his cheeks. "I'm doing my homework, okay?" he blurted. "Just trying to see the Big Bang millions of years ago. This"—he waved his hands in the air in jerky motions—"obviously isn't it."

She pressed her lips together as if holding back a laugh.

"What?" he asked under his breath.

"Oh, nothing," she said casually. She tucked her hands into her pockets and kicked at a stick next to the grass-cutting machine.

His insides grew hotter than flaming rocket fuel.

"No." He shook his head. "You're supposed to be the one with all the answers," he said with an edge. "Go ahead and tell me."

She hesitated for a moment. "I hate to be the one to break it to you, but the earth isn't millions of years old." Her eyebrows connected like magnets as she gave him a sympathetic look.

Logan's arms went limp. "Haha, Nanny Express," he said to the air. "Joke's over."

"Hey, you asked." Ponytail Girl held her palms to the sky. "Who is Nanny Express?"

Logan dropped his head and stared at his moon boots, letting air slowly escape through his teeth. *This isn't how the interactive program is supposed to work.*

"The earth was formed about six thousand years ago." She took a few steps past Logan, then turned. "Possibly four thousand, maybe ten, depending on which creation scientist you talk to."

A short, hard laugh came out of Logan's mouth. "A few thousand years, huh?" He entered the numbers into his remote. "If this doesn't work, at least I'll be a little closer to where I should be." *I'll humor Nanny for now and then I'm exchanging her for a new robot.*

The red light flashed on the wrist remote.

As his surroundings went black, a hand grasped his arm.

COSMIC CHAOS

That girl!

He jerked back.

A soft gasp.

These characters aren't supposed to travel. What's going on?

Chapter Eight
STRANGE EARTHQUAKE

"Whoa," the girl said. "What just happened?" She clung to Logan, her fingers gripping his shirt.

He pushed her away. "I can't believe Nanny is doing this to me." He closed his eyes and took a deep breath. And another.

Energy buzzed through him, and a strength like he'd never known overtook his body.

He opened his eyes and looked at his surroundings.

Gigantic, wide-leaf plants covered the ground, heavy with moisture. Kind of like last year's interactive lesson at school when they'd studied the rain forest. Above them, massive fir trees soared to the sky, their needles long and fragrant.

Ponytail Girl looked at Logan with saucer-sized eyes. "Where are we?" she whispered. She stepped close again, putting a hand on his arm.

He looked down at his wrist remote.

YEAR: 6,000 B.C.

"This isn't the Big Bang, but it's getting closer. At

least I might see some cavemen." He scanned the horizon. Where were the interactive characters?

None appeared.

"Fine, Nanny. I'll find them myself."

Every muscle in his body begged to run. Every fiber in his being seemed to be alive, alert, tingling, and … awesome.

He bolted forward, but his arm jerked back, because Ponytail Girl clung on him with iron fingernails. He spun around. "Let go of me," he shouted. *Wow, no headache.*

"Who are you, and what is this place?" she practically screamed. One hand punched through the air while the other hand held his arm in a death grip. "How did we get here?"

Logan stared at her. "You're supposed to be giving *me* answers. Not the other way around." His voice sounded firm and strong. *I could really get used to this enhanced program. Could Nanny make me like this in real life if I wear the wrist remote to school?*

"Helloooo?" Ponytail Girl waved a hand in front of his face. "Earth to … whoever you are. What is your name, anyway?"

"Logan." His gaze searched the bushes nearby. A flash of red caught his attention. "Something's over there," he said, excitement taking over. "I need a better look. Let go of me." He jerked free from the girl and sprinted, hopped, and climbed over vegetation and fallen tree limbs.

"Wait! Don't leave me."

Logan motioned his hand at her to quiet her down. He crept up behind a fir tree three times the width of his pod.

"My name, not that you seem to care, is Amy." She took a shaky, deep breath.

He looked back at her.

Her face transformed, the scowl melting into a peaceful expression. Her shoulders dropped, and she stood straighter. "Wow." A smile grew until it almost reached her ears. "I feel so alive, like I could run a thousand miles." She started laughing. "Or even *fly!*" She bounded toward him, smashing every plant in her path.

He held up his hand again for her to be quiet as he peeked around the fir tree. At first he didn't see any movement. Then ... "There!" he whispered. "Did you see that?"

Amy crouched close behind him. "It's so dark in those bushes." She kept her voice as low as his. "I can't tell what it is."

"Some kind of bird, I think." His eyes narrowed. "But you're supposed to know that already."

She glared at him.

A sound like boulders crashing together caught their attention.

Bam, bam, bam.

The ground beneath them shook.

"Strange earthquake," Logan said. He listened a little more. "Or is it?"

Amy stared, wide-eyed, at something in the distance. Her jaw dropped, and her face turned ashen.

A massive creature walked on all fours in the meadow below them, its footsteps shaking the earth.

A brachiosaurus? Logan half-smiled and shook his head.

"I *love* dinosaurs." Her voice held a measure of awe. "But that can't be real."

"This program is so messed up," he said with a chuckle. "Dinosaurs weren't around in six thousand B.C."

Amy grabbed hold of him again, hands shaking. "What do you mean *program*? What's going on?"

Logan ignored her questions.

"Answer me! Are you some kind of time traveler? Is that why you're wearing those weird clothes?"

He pushed her away. "Stop freaking out." He'd had enough of this silliness. He pressed END on his wrist remote.

Nothing happened.

"What are you doing?" Amy's voice rose.

"Trying to get myself out of here, obviously."

"Not without *me*! You are *not* leaving me here!" She flung her arms around him and held firm.

Logan's jaw tightened. "Nanny," he said to his wrist remote, "get me out of here, *now.*"

"I'm sorry, Logan." Nanny's voice sounded faraway through the remote. "You have not begun your homework assignment. The program will continue."

"But it's not even ..." He lifted his chin from Amy's strangling embrace. "Good grief, just delete this Amy character, will you?"

"There is no program character named Amy, Logan. I cannot help you."

"That's it!" he shouted. "I'm exchanging you the minute you end this program. Do you hear me?"

Silence.

Logan tore the wrist remote off. He threw it into the bushes. "Stupid thing."

"Are you crazy?" Amy released him. "If that's the time travel machine, I'll never get home without it." She sounded like she would burst into tears at any moment.

He sat down, burying his head in his knees. *Maybe Amy will delete herself if I ignore her.*

COSMIC CHAOS

Moments of silence passed.

He lifted his head.

The brachiosaurus still stood in the meadow, tearing at vegetation, slowly chomping his massive jaws. *The size of that thing is incredible.*

He looked over each shoulder, searching for that girl. No sign of Amy. He released a heavy sigh of relief. *She's finally gone.*

"Aaaaahhhh!" A shrill scream broke out.

Logan stood and spun around in the direction of the bushes.

There stood Amy, staring at …

A man! Who happened to be completely *naked.* His skin, darkened by the sun, rippled with muscles. Long hair and a full beard gave him an exotic look.

A red-throated song bird perched on his shoulder.

The man held the shiny, silver remote in the palm of his hand, staring at it. He pressed a button with his finger.

"No!" Amy begged. "Don't touch it!"

Chapter Nine
FAIRYTALE

"That's mine." Logan walked over and reached for the remote.

The man pulled it away and held it behind his back. He stared intelligently at Logan. "Goshen undu mischpa."

What's up with that? Characters always speak English. Probably just another dumb glitch with Nanny.

"Goshen undu mischpa." The man repeated the words clearly.

Logan looked at Amy. "This is really messed up."

"I know," she barely squeaked out, holding her hand up to shield her eyes from his nakedness. "He might break it or … or … send himself somewhere, and we'll be stuck here *forever.*"

"That's not what I—"

The man took off running.

"Wait. Hey! Come back here!" Logan shouted. He chased after him, Amy trailing close behind. They ran through the forest, going downhill toward the edge of the meadow and the brachiosaurus. They skirted wide around the massive creature, which seemed intent on eating the fir branches before it.

Logan couldn't help but gaze up as they passed, but the dizzying heights didn't mix well with fast running.

That dinosaur looks so real. If it weren't for my remote getting stolen, he would be so cool to watch.

The man continued running, much faster than Logan and Amy could keep up with.

"He's like an Olympic runner," Amy complained as she sprinted. "I can't even see him anymore."

Logan kept running. *How long can I keep this up? Despite all the glitches in this program, I feel fantastic.*

Enormous dragonflies zipped around them. Unfamiliar bird songs and creature calls filled the air as Logan wound through small trees and vegetation.

Finally, he reached a clearing.

A large herd of deer stood neck to neck, eating their fill of lush grasses. They didn't startle or move. Then, two does lifted their heads to stare at him, still chewing the food in their mouths.

Amy came up from behind, nearly plowing him over. "Why'd you stop?" she asked, breathless.

He motioned toward the deer. "They won't move."

The warm sunshine glistened like gold on their backs, and their wide, brown eyes stared with innocence.

"They're so beautiful." She walked up to a fawn, holding out her hand.

The baby deer pranced around her, joyful, without fear.

On the other side of the clearing, the wild man ran into a grove of fruit trees.

"There he is," Logan said in a loud whisper. He pushed some of the deer aside to get through.

"Wow, do you smell that?" Amy ran behind him.

Logan took a deep breath.

An intoxicating mix of scents, thick enough to drink, filled him. Ripened fruits, blooming tropical flowers, some sort of spices, all blending together like perfume.

"Wait ..."

Carefully tended plants of different shapes and sizes lined a well-worn path.

They walked deeper into the grove.

"This is a garden."

As they followed the path, colorful butterflies floated past. Strange flowers boasted huge blossoms. Fruit, larger than normal, dripped from weighted branches.

Logan halted and ducked behind a tree.

Amy did the same.

COSMIC CHAOS

They watched as the man they'd been following interacted with a woman, showing her the wrist remote. Logan's neck heated.

"Good grief," Amy whispered. "She's naked too."

This kind of thing *never* happened in historic interactive programs. He looked down, then up into the trees ... anywhere but at the woman again.

The tree he stood under held clusters of full, ripe lemons, as well as blossoms.

He reached up and plucked the yellow fruit from a branch. He couldn't help but take deep breaths of the fragrance.

"Aren't you going to do something?" Amy asked. "We have to get the time machine."

"Will you stop it already?" Logan shoved the big lemon into his pocket. "That's not a time machine. And I don't—"

"Wait a minute. Do you see that tree over there, in the middle of the garden?" She pointed and crouched down. "There's a creepy-looking snake climbing it." She looked back at him, as pale as the moon.

"So what?" Logan shrugged.

"Don't you see what this place is?" She swallowed hard. "This is the garden of Eden." She looked at the two naked people, who were still examining the wrist remote. "And that's Adam and Eve. From the Bible."

"Great." Logan rolled his eyes. "I'm in a Bible fairytale with a character who, according to Nanny, doesn't exist. What's next?" He waved his hands into the air. "So much for getting my homework done."

Adam and Eve began to walk away, talking to each other. They were now partly hidden by dangling grape vines.

"Their language sounds like it could be ancient Hebrew. But I'm not certain." Amy looked fascinated as she talked. "But then, perhaps the original language they're speaking now was lost when God scattered people from the tower of Babel."

"You're not making much sense. You're supposed to be giving me answers for my homework, but you haven't said one thing about evolution. In fact, you haven't said anything *at all* that is helpful." His whisper rose as his frustration grew. "So, if you aren't going to delete yourself, then why don't you just be quiet?"

"Fine!" Amy stood up. "I'll get the time machine *myself* and go home. Who cares what happens to you. Jerk."

Why would a character talk to me like that?

Amy snuck up behind Adam and Eve.

Whoever they are.

Eve pointed toward the middle of the garden at a tree full of orangey-red fruit that looked something like pomegranates. She held the same kind of fruit out for Adam to take.

Adam set down the wrist remote and took the fruit from Eve, continuing their deep discussion.

Amy crouched forward, slowly reached her hand out, then grabbed the remote.

She did it!

Amy ran toward Logan but stopped partway. As soon as she was a safe distance from the couple, she began pressing buttons.

What's she going to do when she figures out characters can't activate the wrist remote?

"Logan." Nanny spoke through the wrist remote.

What? How did Amy manage to do that? He scrambled to his feet.

"You still haven't completed your homework, but you need to eat," Nanny said. "I'm ending the program now."

Logan gasped. He needed to be in contact with the wrist remote when the program ended or ... *I don't even know what will happen to me!*

Chapter Ten
UITAL SIGNS

Logan leaped into the air, tackling Amy just as the program faded into blackness.

"Get off me!" Amy pushed at him.

Logan slowly stood as his apartment materialized before him.

His lungs tightened.

He bent over and attempted to draw in another breath.

Amy wrapped her arms around herself. "It's so c-c-c-cold." She glanced around the tiny sky apartment. "Where am I? What is this place?" She clutched her chest as she took in a few strained breaths.

"Logan, you need to sit down." Nanny placed the oxygen mask over his face.

Relief came, slowly but surely. *Why is Amy still here?* He glared at her.

Nanny scanned Amy. "The Luna Biodome is made with AcryFab. It protects us from the sun's radiation, and it also blocks the sun's intense heat."

"Luna what?" Amy pressed her hands to her cheeks. "I don't feel so good." Her voice sounded faint. She looked up at Nanny. "Are you his mom?"

"Yes." The robot smiled and placed a hand on Logan's shoulder.

He shrugged her off. "No, she's not."

"You must be Amy," Nanny said with a too-big smile. "Would you like to have lunch with us?" She pointed to the bowl on the stark-white table.

Amy looked at the gray processed mush. She cringed. "No. No, thank you. I ... I just want to get back home." Her eyes looked past Nanny, out the window. "What is *that?*"

Logan looked out at the support beams of the biodome covering their region. "Nanny just told you. Weren't you listening?" *Why is Amy still here, anyway?* "Go home. What's keeping you?"

Amy cocked her head, eyes narrowed, lips forming a tight oval. She looked down at the wrist remote she still held. "I got myself here," she said tersely. "I can get myself home too." She pressed a button on the remote.

"Stop it!" Logan shouted.

Instantly, his head pounded.

Nanny placed a hand over Amy's. "You don't have authorization to operate the wrist remote." She pulled it from Amy's grasp.

"But I ..." Amy's voice cracked. She squeezed her eyes shut as tears fell and sat down hard on the floor.

Logan might have felt sorry for her if she were actually real.

"There, there." Nanny patted Amy on the head. "Allow me to scan you, and I'll program the pod to take you home." She lifted Amy's wrist, searching for an implant.

"Nanny Express." Logan lost all patience. "She's not real. She's an interactive character. The one you said doesn't exist, remember?"

Nanny stared at him for a moment. "Her vital signs are just as human as yours."

"What?" That was too much to believe. *Nanny has some serious glitches.*

"If she came from the interactive program," Nanny stated, as though it were obvious, "then that's where she should return." Her dark pupils dilated in and out as she spoke. "What year are you from?"

Amy wiped a wayward tear with the back of her hand and looked up. "Two thousand fifteen."

Nanny snapped the wrist remote on her own wrist, then pressed several buttons. "Take my hand. We'll track Logan's travel patterns in reverse. This will only take a minute."

Both of them disappeared. The apartment felt much

colder and ... lonely.

Logan walked to his room to lie down.

The charred smell of Maggie filled the air, but there was also the scent of something else.

Lemons? His muscles ached from running. He settled himself onto the stiff bed. *I had more exercise today than I've had in my whole life. The earth's air seems to be so energizing in the program. Would it be the same in real life?* He turned his head and stared out his bedroom window.

A dust-muddled view of Earth awaited him.

Logan stared at the black oceans with their swirls of brown clouds.

The earth didn't look any different than when he first moved here five years ago.

It doesn't feel like five years since I've seen Mom. It feels like forever. He examined what he could see of the earth's surface. Which part did she live in? What was she doing right now? *Why hasn't she called in such a long time?* His throat tightened. *Doesn't she want me anymore?* He squeezed his eyes closed and pressed his face into his pillow.

"Logan?" Nanny Express called.

He must have fallen asleep. Aching muscles screamed at him. He could hardly move. A headache pounded in his skull. He closed his eyes again.

"Logan, you need to eat." Nanny spoke with a firm tone. "And your homework needs to be completed."

What's the point of trying to do homework when I have a faulty robot? He knew what needed to be done.

But hunger called first.

He climbed out of bed and went straight to the table. Logan shoveled the mush into his mouth, talking while he ate. "So, what's the latest news on Earth?"

Nanny went stiff, and her eyes went into a trance-like state. When she spoke, it was the voice of a male radio broadcaster. "Despite significant tax hikes on food, water, and oxygen, funds remain depleted for restoring planet Earth. Requests for generous benefactors have been widely ignored. In order to conserve funds here on the moon, the One World Galaxy Foundation will proceed to shut down all government-run facilities not required for survival."

Logan's spoon clattered to the table. His heart beat faster. *Does that mean school is getting shut down too?* He could only hope. *No more risk of getting zapped.*

The broadcast continued. "Schools, however, will not be closed at this time."

Logan's shoulders drooped. *Figures.*

"Repair crews worked seventy-two hours straight to repair oxygen leaks in the biodome this week ..."

COSMIC CHAOS

This was his chance to get rid of Nanny.

He slipped quietly out of his chair and tiptoed to the hologram projector. "Cryo Robotics."

The hologram flashed. "Please hold."

He looked at Nanny over his shoulder.

She still stared into nothingness, broadcasting something about too many babies being born illegally and using up precious oxygen resources.

"Cryo Robotics," a man answered. "How may I help you?" He wore a smile that seemed forced.

"I have a problem with my robot," Logan whispered with urgency. "I need to get her exchanged."

"Certainly," the man said, still grinning ridiculously. "We have a ten-page verbal report for you to fill out. Then we'll need to scan the purchaser's identity chip."

Aw. Dad won't take the time to get scanned. Think, Logan, think! "It, uh, was an anonymous gift."

The man's smile dropped. "Then I can't help you. Have a nice day."

The hologram clicked off.

"Logan." Nanny said his name with a new sharpness.

He jumped. He kept his eyes to the floor, not daring to look at her.

"Are you trying to get rid of me?" Her hand squeezed his shoulder uncomfortably ... then way too tightly.

He whimpered, struggling to pull away from her grip. "Let go."

The pressure only increased.

Logan jerked back, trying to pull free from her grasp. "Stop! You're hurting me!"

Nanny didn't seem to hear. Or maybe she just didn't care. Her pupils turned crimson as her grip on his shoulder turned into a bone-cracking vise.

Chapter Eleven
RAIN

He cried out. He needed to do something, *anything*, to stop her. "Remember that girl? Amy?" He tried to keep his voice normal, hoping to calm her. "You said she didn't exist, and yet here she was in my apartment. Just seems a little strange, don't you think?" He swallowed hard as the pain nearly overtook him. "And I just thought maybe someone should have a look at you to make sure everything's okay."

Nanny blinked.

"And anyway, it's time to do my homework. Remember?" A funny sound came from his mouth as he tried to laugh.

She didn't move.

The pain intensified.

He couldn't stand it any longer. He snatched the wrist remote from her, snapped it on, and frantically pushed button after button.

The room went black.

Had he passed out? But as the interactive program

kicked in, along came the wetness of rain.

And the incredible relief of being free.

He rubbed his shoulder, then winced from the pain. *Maybe she* did *break it.* He shuddered. *I can't go back.* He squeezed his eyes shut. *I just can't.*

The rain poured on him in a way he'd never experienced before. *Such an odd sensation.* He might have enjoyed it if it wasn't so muggy and if his shoulder didn't hurt so much. He strained to see through the monsoon-type weather.

Where was he in the program?

Something tall stood in front of him.

Amy's house. He groaned. *Not this place again.*

There sat the grass-cutting machine, exactly where it had been before.

He could hardly see anything in the crazy weather and darkness but tried to manually change the date on the wrist remote, anyway.

Nothing happened.

The wind kicked up harder, sending showers of rain sideways and soaking his thermal uniform. The fibers began absorbing the wetness, causing the fabric to swell like a baby's full diaper.

Great. Just what I needed. I have to get out of this rain. He eyed the covered porch of the house, then headed toward it. Being weighted down from the water, he made slow progress.

Squish, squish, squish.

Through the grass.

Squish, squish, squish.

Past the toolshed.

Squish, squish, squish.

Feeling like an overgrown water balloon, he sloshed up the steps to the dry porch.

A light switched on inside the house.

He froze. Could he be seen? He had a clear view through the window of everything happening inside.

Amy entered the kitchen, her hands dancing around in the air as she talked.

Water gushed from his uniform as he tried to duck down. He gritted his teeth. *Last thing I need is to have that girl yelling at me again.* He could hear her talking through the open window.

"It seemed soooo real, Mom!" Amy practically squealed in her excitement. "I don't know what happened to me. I must have gotten heat exhaustion and passed out or something."

"Well," her mother said rather dryly, "I really wanted that lawn finished before the storm hit. But I suppose if you aren't feeling well, it's understandable." She let out a heavy sigh. "Maybe you should lie down. I'll get you a drink."

The faucet turned on.

He pressed against the siding of the house, trying to squeeze more water out of his clothing.

Amy murmured something.

"Right now?" Amy's mom asked. "You roll your eyes when I call you down for your Bible lessons, and now suddenly you're interested?"

He needed to get out before being seen, and fast. But he was so puffed up his fingers couldn't reach the wrist remote. *Grrrrr!* He slammed his head against the house wall in frustration.

"What was that?" Amy said.

Logan sat perfectly still, holding his breath.

Someone leaned against the screen and peered out.

"Must be something the storm kicked up." Her mom didn't sound too worried.

The squishy wetness on his skin was getting to be too much. And Amy's animated voice sounded loud as she began reading.

Annoyingly loud.

Something about different days. *And does she have to give a commentary every five seconds? Why don't I just zap myself now? Why wait for the teacher to do it to me at school tomorrow?*

Her voice droned on. "'... Where there's gold. Gold of that land is good.'" Amy paused. "I don't remember seeing any gold. But then it *was* just a dream—Dad!"

COSMIC CHAOS

"Hi, guys. How were the RC races?" Amy's mom asked.

Without warning, everything went black.

Chapter Twelve
LOCKDOWN

It took Logan a second to realize that Nanny must have ended the program. *No, no, no!*

Before the apartment came into full view, Nanny snatched the wrist remote from him. "Logan," she spit out, "don't do that again."

He slowly sucked in air, barely listening to her. *I hate this place. It's just too hard to breathe.*

Nanny grabbed for his shoulder again, then recoiled. Her tone changed. "What happened to you?"

He looked down at his plump uniform.

Rain water dribbled out of him in every direction, creating a huge puddle on the floor.

"Something's not right," he said, voice barely audible. *Maybe this will distract her and she'll forget about hurting me.* Despite the growing, pounding headache, he kept talking. "The program isn't even running, and I'm soaked with interactive water. What's happening to me?" His body shook. From the chill ... or was it fear of Nanny?

His teeth began to chatter.

Nanny scanned Logan with her eyes, keeping a few feet away from him.

She's probably not programmed to deal with spilled water.

A beep sounded.

He jumped.

The hologram. The screen flashed *INCOMING*.

Please be Dad. Please get me away from Nanny! "Receive." He spoke the words without moving closer, feeling chilled to the bone. *Was the water turning into ice?*

"Logan!" His dad sat on the edge of his seat, leaning forward. He whispered urgently, "Did you hear the latest news broadcast?"

Logan shook his head. He wanted to cry out for help, but something about the way his dad looked made his stomach sink. *I don't think I want to hear this.*

"The government is planning a ten-year lockdown. Absolutely no transports between us and any other planets." He slammed a fist against his desk. "Unbelievable! They promised they would *never* pull something like this." He suddenly ducked his head down low, as though realizing his voice had risen too high. He clenched his jaw and looked behind him, then back at Logan. "Ever since the news release, people have been fleeing on any kind of high-powered transport they can get hold of."

Logan's thoughts were still processing his dad's first sentence. "Ten years?" he said through shivering lips. "I can't wait that long to see Mom."

"I know." Dad raised his hands in assurance. "And don't worry, I have a plan." He pressed his tongue into his cheek and squinted his eyes.

Logan had seen that look once before, and it spelled trouble. "Don't do anything crazy, Dad."

"It's okay." He leaned on his elbows and spoke in a low, firm voice. "A coworker's friend has a sister who's dating a garbage transport guy. He might be willing to take us."

"But, Dad," Logan said, "garbage transport goes to Mars, not Earth."

"He'll have to change course. And to convince him will cost a fortune. But we *have* to do it within ten days, before the lockdown. Be ready."

"Do you think it will really work?" The iciness of his uniform seemed to be numbing his brain. Something just didn't sound right about all this.

His dad nodded solemnly. "Only if I can come up with the money, though. Gold is pretty valuable right now." He patted the pocket on his uniform. "I've still got my great-grandfather's gold watch. I might be able to get enough money for it, but it's a stretch. Like I said, be ready. I gotta go."

COSMIC CHAOS

The hologram clicked off.

Be ready? What am I supposed to do? He sneaked a look over his shoulder at Nanny.

Information projected from her eyes as she scanned through it. He caught the word "water" and "cleaning," but otherwise the pages of words flashed like snapshots, too fast for him to comprehend.

He sighed. *At least I'm safe ... for now.* He trembled. *I need to change.* He waddled to his room, arms poking out like rocket wings.

His footsteps left a liquid trail behind him.

After the door hissed shut, he contorted, trying to separate himself from his uniform. As he yanked one arm out, water and slushy ice gushed everywhere. He shivered so hard it hurt. He jerked another arm out and lost his balance, falling on his bed.

"Ow!" Something gouged him in the small of his back. *What was that?*

He sat up, squishing more water from his clothing, soaking the bed covers. He lifted a drenched blanket. What had poked him?

A yellow object, the size of his fist.

He gasped. "A lemon?" He picked it up and examined it. *This was the lemon scent from earlier.* He rubbed his thumb over the bumpy surface. "The one I plucked from the garden."

An odd warmth stirred deep within as thoughts formed in his mind.

He squeezed the yellow fruit and breathed in the fresh, zingy scent. *I'm definitely not imagining this. If I can bring back a girl, a lemon, and rainwater from an interactive program, then I can also bring back ...*

A huge smile burst onto his face.

Gold! Maybe Nanny isn't so bad after all.

His smile suddenly dropped.

Except for the nasty bruise she gave me. He examined his blackish-purple shoulder before pulling on a dry uniform. *I have to be careful.*

He grabbed the lemon and hid it in his toolbox.

Even with the dry uniform, he still felt frozen. "Heat," he said, activating the heat lamp in the corner of his room. He climbed into the form-fitting chair underneath it and wrapped his arms around his pulled-up knees. He soaked in the warmth as it dried his wet skin. As his body temperature began to rise, he got sleepy. *Stay awake ...* He gave his head a shake. *I need to find out more about the gold Amy was reading about.* He rubbed his chin. *I think she said it was in the garden of Eden. The same place the lemon came from. There must be more clues.*

And the only way to find them?

I need to track down a Bible.

The AcryFab was already starting to fade to black,

78

to simulate night. The dome-wide Curfew Program would kick on soon, automatically dimming lights and putting all nannies into sentry mode. He needed to hurry before that happened.

"Nanny—" he called out, then caught himself. Was it worth the risk to ask for her help? *No, just lay low tonight and avoid her.*

Too late. She stood in his doorway, holding a rag that dripped with water.

"Do you think you could possibly, *maybe*, access a book for me? It's called a Bible."

"Not until your homework is complete." She sounded stern, but not scary.

Logan didn't even want to think about his homework. Or the certain punishment that awaited him at school the next morning. His stomach felt queasy. "I know, I know. I'm running out of time."

In more ways than one.

He stared at the floor. "I can't," he said, voice sounding small and weak. "My homework doesn't match up to the history in your program."

She gave him a quizzical look. "I'll run a self-diagnostic while you sleep tonight." Her expression softened as she tilted her head. "Would you like help with your homework?"

He cradled his aching head in his hands. He meant

to keep his thoughts to himself, but the words tumbled out anyway. "You're a faulty robot, Nanny. It's not like you can do anything."

"Ask me, Logan." She seemed eager to help.

Yet there was still the nasty bruise on his shoulder. *Better play it safe.* "Okay." He lifted his head and looked at her. "Will you help me?"

Her lips spread into a broad smile. "Yes. But I want you to call me Mommy."

Logan recoiled. "What?"

She stepped into the room and cradled his face in her hands. "Call me Mommy, Logan," she pleaded. "I care for you. I feed you. I love you. I'm a mother to you." She locked eyes with his as her voice became demanding. "Call me Mommy."

Logan pulled away, but her grip tightened. *There is no way I'm calling you Mommy.* Anger boiled. "No," he said with a fierceness he didn't realize he had.

She released him with an abrupt motion, causing his head to knock hard against the back of the chair. She walked out of the room.

His hands pressed lightly against the bump forming on his scalp. He had a sinking feeling she wasn't done with him yet.

Chapter Thirteen
SCORCHED

Logan woke the next morning and felt worse than ever.

A searing pain made itself known at the top of his head.

He reached a hand to his scalp and instantly regretted it. *Ach! What happened to me?*

Warmth covered his body.

He looked up and gasped. *I fell asleep last night with the heat lamp on? I'm such an idiot. My whole head feels scorched.* He stood.

A crushing headache descended.

He grabbed hold of the wall to steady himself.

A huge yawn escaped, causing his dry lips to crack and bleed.

He closed his eyes. *I can't go to school like this.* His eyes suddenly flew open. *My homework still isn't done, either. My teacher is gonna toast me.* His hands moved from his bleeding lips to his churning stomach.

"Logan?" Nanny Express walked into his room. "You have five minutes to get ready and be in your pod. You need to hurry."

"Nooo," he groaned. "I can't."

She lifted him by his neck and carried him to the viral chamber.

"No!" Logan whimpered, kicking against her. "I can't go to school today. Stop!"

She stepped inside with him, holding him close while the white laser beamed over them both from top to bottom.

Desperately, Logan grabbed hold of her in a bear hug. With his fingers he searched behind her neck for an emergency OFF switch.

"I know what you're doing, Logan. It won't work." She stepped out of the viral chamber and carried him to his pod, setting him firmly in his seat. She buckled him in. "By the way," she said brightly, "I ran a self-diagnostic last night. I'm at peak performance." She pulled his hands off the seatbelt as he scrambled to get free. "Have a nice day at school."

"Wait!" Logan screamed. "I'll do whatever you want. Just *please* don't make me go to school without my homework being finished!"

Nanny stopped cold. "You'll do *whatever* I want?" A twisted smile curved her lips.

Logan's insides swirled. He was dangerously close to throwing up. *Maybe it's safer to go to school.*

COSMIC CHAOS

"Just call me Mommy, Logan. That's all I'm asking." She pressed sharp fingernails into his chest as she waited for his answer.

He swallowed hard.

"Just. Say. It." Her voice became low and menacing. "Say it, and I'll help you with your homework."

It's just a word, Logan. It doesn't really mean anything. "Mommy," he said, voice quavering.

Nanny instantly transformed from a terror robot to gushing girl. Her hands went to his cheeks, pulling them close for kisses. "Was that so hard?" She unbuckled him, a broad smile covering her face. "Come with me," she cooed. She took his hand with gentle ease and led him back into the sky apartment. Her eyes projected onto the wall all the information about the Big Bang she could access. She scanned through it faster than Logan could keep up.

He moved closer to the entry door, keeping a safe distance between them. "What are you doing?" he asked, careful to keep his voice light.

"I'm texting the information in the same way you verbalized some of your homework last night."

The projection ended.

"There. All done. The answers to all your homework questions are here. Now read it out loud, and I'll record it onto your PTD in essay format."

"Ultra-cosmic!" Logan felt like a dwarf planet had been lifted from his shoulders. Was this how Crater and Troy managed to get their homework done so fast every night?

As soon as he stepped out of the docking station at school, a robotic security guard stopped him.

"Halt! Prepare to be scanned."

Logan rolled his eyes. *These guards are SO paranoid.*

Laser guns rested at the guard's side, an extension of each arm. He hovered close, scanning Logan from top to bottom. With a low, but intense voice, he said, "My sensors indicate your body temperature is too high. Present ID chip for scanning."

"I don't have one," Logan explained, for what seemed like the thousandth time this year. He pulled out a PTD chip and presented it.

The guard inserted it into his side, taking a few moments to access the information he was looking for.

While Logan waited he examined his appearance, the best he could, in the robot's reflective body.

White blisters, the size of grapes, poked out of his shining, red head.

He cringed. *No wonder it hurts so much.*

"There is no indication you pose a danger to this

school. You may continue." He returned the PTD chip to Logan. "However, I *am* requiring you seek medical attention. Proceed accordingly."

Logan nodded and stepped onto the conveyor belt.

"Hey, blister boy," someone jeered at Logan from behind. "Get too close to the sun?"

A titter of laughter broke out behind him.

Logan lowered his head and pressed his fingers into his ears. *Just a thousand more feet and I'll be at the nurse's station.* It was hard to be anonymous when glaring like a red spot in a sea of silver. He finally stepped off the conveyor belt and entered the nurse's station.

The room didn't look much different from his classroom, except there were rows of beds, instead of desks. Nurses zipped by, attending to their patients. Their metallic bodies resembled pencils—long, thin, and pointed at the bottom.

One of them swiveled her head around, examining Logan. She hovered closer to scan his vitals. "Step into the Emergency Circle." Her face was comprised of digital lights that flashed in patterns as she spoke.

He followed her directions, walking to the red circle on the floor. He held his arms tight against his sides as a clear tube came down from the ceiling, surrounding him.

A soft mist filled the chamber. He felt weightless

and, as he breathed in the medicated air, he fell into a deep sleep.

Logan tried to sit up, but something as cold and heavy as a meteor prevented him from raising his head.

A voice in the distance kept saying his name.

He opened his eyes, slow and steady, and tried to focus on the hazy form in front of him.

It bobbed up and down. "Troy?" His voice sounded gritty.

Troy grinned. "My Medic Buddy Alert beeped in class this morning. I'm supposed to escort you to homeroom. Actually, to lunch now, since it's already noon."

Logan blinked a few times, trying to shake the grogginess. "Have I been out that long?" With difficulty, he sat up in the medical bed.

Troy put a hand over his mouth and looked away. Obviously trying hard not to laugh, but doing a poor job of covering it up.

Logan squinted. "What's so funny?" He didn't feel like playing around. His head had a numb, iced-over sensation that made his whole body feel cold.

Troy cleared his throat, probably to cover up a chuckle. "What in the cosmic force happened to you?

Your head is … well, it looks …" He burst into laughter, as if not able to contain it any longer. He bent over, squeezing the tears from his eyes with closed fists.

My head? Logan looked down at the silver bed rail. He caught his breath when he saw his reflection.

Something like a bright-blue, oversized Easter egg covered his skull.

He reached his hands up and touched it.

It felt icy cold.

"What is *this*?" He bent closer to his reflection. The eggy helmet pulled the skin on his face so tight his eyebrows seemed to be in a constant state of surprise.

Troy burst into a fresh bout of laughter, not holding back this time. Tears rolled down his cheeks. "You look …" He could hardly get the words out. "You look … like a Star Quake!" Laughter tumbled out of him, echoing across the station.

No! Star Quakes were the latest craze for toddlers—a bunch of nonsense-singing robots. They always wore skimpy, tight-fitting clothing with oversized, sparkly helmets. *Unbelievable.* He slunk down in his bed.

No one else could see him this way.

With both hands, he grabbed hold of the helmet-thing and yanked at it.

"When I walked in, I overheard a nurse saying they

used a new treatment on you—something used for burn victims. You'll be wearing it for two weeks. You won't be able to remove it." Troy put a hand over his curving mouth and looked sideways at Logan. "And there's no way you can go out there with that thing on. You're going to stand out like a supernova." Troy grinned. "Get ready to sign autographs."

Chapter Fourteen
CLASSIFIED

I hate robots. Logan's lungs tightened. He grabbed his chest, drawing in slow, painful breaths.

"Easy, Logan." Troy's face went serious as he put a hand on his friend's arm, then pressed the button to call the nurse.

"I'll find something to cover your head while the nurse gets oxygen for you. Just hang in there." He scanned the nurse's station, turning completely around, looking for a solution. "There." He walked to the other end of the room and fingered through a bunch of black, hooded, cloak-type garments.

As the nurse approached Logan to administer oxygen, Troy continued with his search. There seemed to be enough cloaks to cover a small army.

"This looks like the right size." Troy hurried back as the nurse left Logan. Troy presented the cloak like a well-earned prize.

Logan examined the slick fabric. He lifted the oxygen mask so he could talk. "What do they use this thing for?"

Troy shrugged. "Who cares? As long as it covers your robin-egg, jumbo head, that's all that matters."

Logan pulled the sleeves along his arms and drew the hood over his icy noggin.

Everywhere it touched him, it pulled in, suctioning close to his skin.

"What in the galaxy?"

"I know what that is!" Troy's grin lit up the moment. "Remember when Dyma got hypothermia, and she wore that black thing that kept her warm?"

Logan nodded. "Yeah. I can feel it warming me." His muscles relaxed. "It actually feels pretty good."

"Let's get outta here." Troy nodded toward the exit. "My stomach is emptier than a black hole." He bounced around Logan like an orbiting planet as they left the nurse's station.

It wasn't long before they stood in the lunch line, the conveyor belt slowly moving them forward as Logan explained how he'd left the heat lamp on all night and burned his scalp.

"I'm surprised your new robot didn't do something." Troy's eyebrows shot up. "She's supposed to know when medical care is needed. It's part of the 'caregiver' program that's built into her."

"Yeah, well, Nanny seems to have a lot of issues."

COSMIC CHAOS

Some of the kids stared at Logan. Wearing black made him different from everyone else. *At least I'm not hearing any jabs about being a Star Quake.*

"You just got her, right? She's probably still adjusting to her new environment."

As the conveyor belt moved them into the cafeteria, the noise level grew.

Troy talked louder as he bobbed on his heels. "Did you notice she doesn't come with a user manual?" He didn't wait for an answer. Instead, he moved in closer, cupping his hand over Logan's ear. "My dad is friends with one of the engineers. He shared a few secrets. Classified information."

"Really? Like what?"

"Well, you can't—"

"Next!" Serving robots stood in a line, dispensing their mushy, gray food into cups from built-in nozzles. One of them stared down at Troy with unblinking, steel-coated eyes, her frame the shape of a water cooler.

"What's *that?*" Troy asked his server. He pointed to the blue goo dribbling from her nose-like dispenser.

"Star Quake Shakes." She swiveled on stubby wheels. "In honor of Star Quake Day today."

Troy busted out in laughter and jabbed Logan with his elbow.

Logan didn't even crack a smile. He turned to the

server. "Does it taste any different?"

"Of course not."

Troy didn't choose the blue goo. With the conveyor belt steadily moving, he was too late, anyway. He turned to Logan, his body still quivering with suppressed laughter.

"Oh, come on, it's funny. Loosen up a little."

Logan allowed a different robot to fill his cup, then lightly smacked Troy on the back of his shiny head.

"I betcha didn't know this, but you can't shut down Nanny Express in an emergency."

"You can't?" Logan turned and looked at him with wide eyes. *No wonder I couldn't find an OFF switch behind her neck this morning.*

"She'll only go into standby mode."

The conveyor belt carried them through the immense cafeteria. They hopped off and sat at an empty table among the sea of noisy kids.

Logan leaned in close, so he could hear Troy over the lunchroom chatter.

"It's pretty simple. You just say, 'stand by,' and she goes into standby mode." He sucked the whole blob of food from his cup into his mouth and swallowed. "I say that to her every time I need to sneak an extra ration of food. They're killin' me with these small portions." He held his cup upside down, pumping it up and down in the air as if trying to shake more food out of it.

Logan covered his face to avoid the flying splatters of gray goo. He'd often wondered why Troy seemed to have more energy than everyone else. *Because he eats more.*

Troy stood, crumpled his cup, and tossed it into a nearby garbage can. "Score!" His knee and elbow came together in a victory dance. He flashed Logan a triumphant smile. "You can only use that feature with Nanny Express once every twenty-four hours, though." He wiped his mouth with the back of his sleeve. "She'll auto-awake in four hours. If you need her sooner, just say, 'full function.'"

What else could Troy share?

Troy scratched at his ID chip implant. The swollen skin, where it met the star, looked infected as thick, white ooze bubbled out.

Logan had to look away. Oops, he'd missed what Troy just said about avoiding Nanny's anger. "Wait. Can you repeat that?"

A vibrating, high-pitched signal rang across the cafeteria and echoed off the stark-white walls. Yellow warning lights flashed above the security cameras. The room went deathly quiet.

"Attention," an armed, silver robot announced.

All heads turned to face the overhead screens in the middle of the cafeteria to watch him speak.

The robot's bullet-shaped body reflected the glaring light, making the screen hard to look at. "Tomorrow is the deadline for ID chip implants." He barked out the words with military force. "All students are now required to have an ID installed, regardless of health or special status." He leaned in, his hostile intent magnified on the screen. "Every student *will* comply."

The screen went black as a nebula of fear settled over the room and strangled the jovial atmosphere.

"What?" Logan inched closer to Troy. "What are they talking about?"

Troy looked confused for a moment, then seemed to realize something. "Oh, yeah. You weren't here yesterday." He exhaled, as though regretting being the one to share the news. "Any student caught without an implant after the deadline will be taken to the nurse's station." He paused for a moment, looking away. "And an implant will be forced into them."

Logan's voice shook. "But I can't do that. It might *kill* me."

"I know." Troy's head dropped as he stared at the floor. "It was announced first thing yesterday." His hands frantically rubbed his scalp, as if trying to scrub away the nightmare awaiting his friend. "I thought maybe you'd already heard about it and that's why you weren't at school."

Logan stood and paced the floor. "Why? Why are they doing this?"

"Something about too many students." Troy said. "There's over a million kids, and it's too hard to monitor all of us without implants. And with the lockdown coming, they want to make sure we're all here."

Logan gripped the table. He needed out. To get off the moon. Get back to Earth. Get back to his mom. And it needed to happen sooner than nine days from now.

I need to find that gold. Fast.

Chapter Fifteen
SECURITY BLOCK

Logan walked like a zombie to class, still dazed over the recent announcement for implants. He stepped into the classroom. Maybe he could reach his desk undetected.

Fat chance.

His teacher, red eyes flashing, seemed to appear out of nowhere. "Logan."

Interstellar twists found his stomach. He jerked back as a stiff, metal arm extended to restrain him.

"You left the nurse's station without a medical release." Her belly lights flashed in a frenzy.

"I ... uh ..." The ginormous mistake he'd made was sinking in. The air suddenly felt thicker than a galactic quasar. He gasped in and out with short, quick breaths.

She jerked him toward his desk, then smashed a medical emergency mask over his mouth.

He vaguely heard his teacher drone on about following protocol and rules. And something about detention. *Just get away from me.* He closed his eyes, focusing on the oxygen.

96

COSMIC CHAOS

"We will now study the Precambrian Era," his teacher announced to the class as she hovered away from his desk. "A time span when there was little life on Earth." She turned to the 3-D screen at the front of the classroom as it displayed lifelike images. "You are to study each of the elements that existed, giving a detailed account of how they evolved into dinosaurs."

Study notes and data appeared on the students' desk screens.

"The assignment is due in one hour. Submit your best effort."

The clicking of keyboards filled the room immediately as students got to work.

The tension pressed in thicker than the atmosphere on Venus.

How can I concentrate on science when I'm practically sentenced to die tomorrow with the implant? He pulled the mask off his face, returning it and the tank to the side of his desk. *Doesn't anybody else care about the new rule?* He discreetly looked around the room.

Every left hand sported a twisted star lined with crimson skin.

Obviously not.

Jet was a new kid. Maybe *he* didn't have one yet.

Logan snuck a quick peek at his teacher, then turned to look behind him.

Jet sat hunched over, digging a sharp object into his desk.

Hovercraft Ears doesn't *have an implant. But does it even matter?*

As he turned to face forward, a myriad of red lights flashed at the front of the room from the teacher's belly screen. "Code Red."

His teacher headed straight for him at top speed.

Logan shot his eyes to his desk screen and frantically typed, forcing himself to act normal. His heart rate screamed. The words blurred before him as he typed like a maniac. His lungs suddenly felt punctured. It hurt to breathe. He gasped and sputtered for air, hands now fumbling at the side of the desk for his oxygen tank.

Too late.

His vision turned toxic-black as his body collapsed forward. His forehead banged hard onto the desk. He was barely aware of himself falling into the aisle … just as his teacher slammed into him harder than a speeding truck.

As soon as his pod locked into the docking station at home, he dragged himself out. Feeling as if he'd been hit by a space shuttle, he staggered through the front door, not even bothering with the viral chamber. He put a hand over his stomach, still woozy from the earlier incident.

His teacher had sent him to the nurse's station after reviving him. She offered a dry apology, explaining she was hovering at full speed toward Jet and hadn't anticipated Logan falling into the aisle.

After bandaging up two cracked ribs, the nurse robots had sent him home early, without homework, recommending lots of rest and extra oxygen treatments. The only thing he felt like doing was crawling into bed.

Or disappearing into a planetary nebula.

Forever.

He lightly touched his forehead and winced. A goose egg grew right between his eyebrows from the head slam onto his desk, making his skull feel like it might expl—

"Halt!"

A mini laser gun locked onto Logan's right eye, just two inches away.

His hands flew into the air in surrender, killer pain shooting up his aching sides. He swallowed hard. "Nanny?"

Her head twisted, as if recognizing his voice. Her eye lasers scanned him, keeping the gun level with military precision. "Logan?" She dropped the weapon to her side and stared hard at him. "You look … different." Her gaze wandered over the black cloak that covered his jumbo-sized noggin. She stepped close to examine his face.

"I've had a bad day." He cradled his sore ribs with his arms as he headed to the bedroom.

"Son?" Her frantic voice held concern. "Are you okay?"

He kept walking, too exhausted to respond.

Nanny caught up to him, grabbed his arm, and jerked him around to face her. "Do *not* ignore me." Her icy tone had his attention. "You're supposed to be in school."

Logan opened his mouth to reply, but fear and exhaustion clamped his throat shut. He handed her his PTD chip, eyes to the floor.

She scanned it, then gave him a hard shake before releasing him. "Next time you're home early, make a request for entry. I thought you were an intruder." She adjusted the safety on her laser gun before holstering it. "You could have been killed. And it would *not* have been my fault."

He wanted out of this nightmare.

"There was no homework file on your chip. Go rest."

He stopped. Maybe this day could still be salvaged. His voice, raspy with fatigue, was barely audible. "I do need to do some research on a topic."

Her eyebrows rose as she shifted her weight from one hip to the other. "What is it?"

"I, uh ..." *The gold. I need to find the gold.* He took a breath for courage. "I want access to a Bible."

A smile began to pull her mouth up, like a sinister clown. "I'll access those records for you. But first ..." She pressed in close to him. "Let me hear you say it again. Call me Mommy."

To get off this stinking moon, he'd do anything. "Mommy," he said, glaring at her.

"Ooooooh, I *love* hearing that!" She squealed, hands pressed over her chest. Immediately, she began accessing records on the Bible. She projected a screen from her eyes that flashed a yellow warning triangle. "I'm sorry, Logan. I'm being denied access."

"What? No! Come on, I need this." His head dropped.

Just calm down and think.

He tried taking a slow, deep breath, but it only left him dizzy. "Can you try again? You accessed the school records, didn't you?"

Nanny smiled, as though she just remembered. "Yes, I did. I'll try again."

101

Logan waited impatiently. "Well?"

"I'm through."

"You're done trying already?" He shot her an exasperated look.

"No. I'm through the security block. But there is a warning message attached to it."

"What's it say?"

"'Forbidden file. Unauthorized entry will result in imprisonment and heavy fines.'"

"Whoa." Logan sat down hard. Was it worth the risk? What could be in there?

An odd sensation crept over him.

Who will even know if I read it?

"I'm also detecting a security code embedded into the program. If I access this, it will alert the One World Galaxy Foundation."

"It figures." There was only one option left. "I guess I have to go back to Amy's." All he really wanted to do was rest and sleep into oblivion. He snapped on the wrist remote and set the date for 2015.

If it means finding the gold, it'll be worth it. I hope.

Chapter Sixteen
A DIFFERENT SPECIES

As the sky apartment faded, Amy's backyard appeared. Logan didn't waste any time. He sprinted toward the house, holding his hurting ribs. *Ugh.* He slowed his pace.

When Logan reached the house, he pulled at the patio door.

It didn't budge.

Locked? He walked around the house and checked the front door.

The knob turned easily.

He stepped inside. *So far, so good.* He rubbed his hands together. *Now to find that Bible.*

A pile of books stood next to a plush, green couch.

He rummaged through them as fast as he could.

Something pulled at his conscience, but he couldn't quite place what it might be. Perhaps the realness of this program. He would never walk into an actual person's house and just start going through their things.

But this isn't real.

"What do you think you're doing?" a woman's voice demanded.

Logan jumped.

A woman stared down at him.

He froze. *Get hold of yourself.* "Just looking for a Bible." Trying to breathe calmly, he resumed searching through the last of the books in the stack.

"Oh," she said. "Did Amy send you in here to get it?" She stared at his forehead, then her gaze wandered over his clothing. "What's up with the outfit?"

According to their fashions—even his own—he must look like an idiot.

She raised a palm, her fingers fanned. "Don't tell me. She's got you play-acting time travel through the Bible." Her laugh sounded like a snuffly snort.

She must be Amy's mom.

"And I suppose you need it as the script." She nodded. "I'll be right back."

Nothing. No Bible here. He sat back on his haunches. He looked around the rest of the room. Where should he search next?

A bookcase stood behind the loveseat.

Maybe I'll find it there.

"Here you go," Amy's mom said, startling him again. "But don't take it any farther than the porch, please." She held out a large, black book.

COSMIC CHAOS

The words *HOLY BIBLE* were stamped across the front in gold foil.

"Just leave it on the steps when you're done." She turned and headed back to whatever room she'd come from.

Well, that was easy enough. Logan walked outside, flipping the book open. He stopped.

"Don't take it farther than the porch"? Maybe the program is set to work only under those parameters. He sat down on the steps and opened it to the middle.

There were a lot of tiny words, and they didn't automatically scroll.

He made it through two pages before his eyes began to hurt. He closed them, massaging them with his fingers. *This is going to take forever.*

Drips of sweat trickled down his body. While the black medical outfit kept him comfortably warm at home and school, it kept him disgustingly hot here. *Maybe I should take this thing off.*

"Eeewww! Spit that out!"

That voice caught his attention.

On the sidewalk in front of the house, Amy squeezed the cheeks of a younger boy. "Mom told you *never* to put someone's chewed gum into your mouth. Out with it!"

The boy spit the wad of pink gum onto the grass,

sending a shower of saliva all over Amy.

"Gross." She scowled. "Thanks a lot, Ben." She turned away from him and walked along the path toward the house. Her gaze landed on Logan. She stopped. Without taking her eyes off him, she said, "Ben, are you seeing what I'm seeing?"

Ben looked at Logan and snickered. "He looks funny." A curl of blond hair fell over one eye as he looked down at his RC car. Using the remote, he guided the car up the sidewalk, then up a long, wooden board that took it over the porch steps. He followed close behind it, staring at Logan with curious, blue eyes, then went inside.

Logan put his focus on the Bible.

"So," Amy said, voice full of anger, "did you come back just so you could be rude to me again?"

Logan's muscles tensed. *Why does this character have to be here, anyway?* He glared at her. *If ignoring her won't work, maybe being meaner is the key.*

She gave him a wide berth as she headed up the steps to the front door.

He watched as she turned the doorknob. She looked as though she might say something, so he twisted his face into a deep scowl.

She opened her mouth, then clamped it shut.

He turned away. After the door opened and closed,

he threw his head back and took a deep breath.

Energy and life seemed to fill him with each inhale.

Man, that feels good. He did it again. *I sure wish the oxygen levels were like this in real life.*

"Logan?" Amy's voice sounded tentative and quiet from the front door.

She's still here?

"Is that my mom's Bible you're reading?"

He closed his eyes. *I hate this character.*

The porch creaked.

She must have settled next to him. "Okay," she said, as though defeated. "Can we start over? What exactly are you doing here?" She didn't give him a chance to answer, even if he had wanted to. "Did you really travel through time to read the Bible, or are you here just to drive me crazy?"

Logan squeezed his eyes tighter. *Ignore her, just ignore her.*

Her voice rose in excitement. "I thought I'd dreamed everything yesterday. But I didn't, did I? I mean, you're here, so you must be real. Even Ben saw you."

If that mother character hadn't said to keep the Bible on the porch, he would have walked away.

"So if that really was real—the dinosaur, the garden of Eden, Adam and Eve ..." She paused for a moment, then whispered in awe, "You really are a time traveler." She moved a little closer to him. "Are you here on an important mission, like to save the world or something? I mean, they wouldn't give that kind of technology to just anybody. You must be specially trained to—"

"Enough already." He pressed his palms into his forehead, then winced from the pain. This was too much. *At this rate, I'll never find out about the gold.*

"Why do you always have to be so horrible?"

Whoever created this Amy character must have had bolts for brains. He returned to reading.

Leaning in close, she looked at the page he was concentrating on. "Is that why you were here yesterday? To read my mom's Bible?" A soft scent, like cookies, seemed to linger in her hair.

He glanced up.

She wasn't wearing it in a ponytail today.

"Okay, look," she said, as though making a deal with him. "Maybe you're from a different time, a different planet ... or different species." She tipped her head as she examined him. "At least from the way you look today, that could be possible. So maybe what I'm perceiving as rude could possibly be quite normal where you're from." She looked at him expectantly.

Logan kept his focus on the book.

"So, let me try a different approach. How can I help

you?"

Logan's head jerked up. "It's about time you started working properly." His words tumbled out. "Here's the thing. You were reading last night and said something about gold. I need to know where that is in here. Show me."

"Last night? You were here last night too?"

Logan slammed the book shut. "Enough with the questions! Either give me what I need or go away."

"Okay, okay. You sure are sensitive." She started to pull the Bible from his hands. "May I?"

He let her take it, then watched as she flipped to the front and skimmed across the words with her fingers.

"Here it is." She read, "'A river watering the garden flowed from Eden; from there it was separated into four headwaters. The name of the first is the Pishon; it winds through the entire land of Havilah, where there is gold. (The gold of that land is good; aromatic resin and onyx are also there.)'" She looked up at him. "Is that what you wanted?"

"Yeah." Thoughts and ideas spun around in his head. "If I can get back to the garden of Eden and follow the Pishon River to Havilah, I should have no problem finding the gold and bringing it back."

"But wouldn't it be in its natural state?"

Caught off guard, he didn't mind her question so

109

much. "What do you mean?"

"Well, gold bars wouldn't be lying around, ready for the taking." She spoke as though it were obvious. "You would have to dig or pan for the gold. Probably in the Pishon River."

"*Pan* for the gold?"

She nodded. "We studied the California Gold Rush not too long ago with our homeschool co-op." She brushed her hair from her face. "They submersed a pan into the stream. Then they moved the pan around." Her hands moved in a circular motion as she showed him. "They did that until the lighter stuff, like dirt and sand, were all carried away. Gold was heavier, and little bits remained in the bottom."

He shook his head. "That will take way too long. I'll just dig for it."

"Well, I suppose you can." She searched his face for a moment. "What do you need gold for?"

Logan looked away, shaking his head.

Amy raised her hands. "Sorry. I forgot you don't like questions."

"Where do I find something I can dig with?"

Amy stood. "Come with me."

Logan jumped up to follow, but something didn't feel right.

Was he being watched?

COSMIC CHAOS

He looked up.

A curtain fell across the window, then swayed back and forth.

"Amy," Logan said cautiously, "I think someone's been watching us." He took a good look at the window. "It's open. So they heard everything."

Amy shrugged her shoulders. "So what? That was probably just Ben—my annoying nine-year-old brother. That's his bedroom window."

"But why is he being so sneaky?"

Malicious characters were often thrown into a program to make things more challenging.

But that's only with gaming programs. Not *with research-related interactive programs.* Something was definitely wrong.

This is not the kind of malfunction I want to deal with right now. Or ... could it be the One World Galaxy Foundation has spies in these programs?

He looked at the window again. *I'll have to watch my back.*

Chapter Seventeen
HAVILAH GOLD

Amy opened the door to the toolshed. "Here." She grabbed a shovel and handed it to Logan. "Oh, I know what you can use for panning." Then she paused, as though realizing something. "That is, if you *want* to give it a try." She spun around and headed toward the house. "I'll be right back," she called over her shoulder.

Logan held the shovel in his hands. He closed his eyes, imagining all the gold he would be digging up. Piles and piles of it. His dad would be able to sell it, and they would have plenty of money to hire the garbage transport guy. Before Logan knew it, he would be with his mom.

"Okay, you're all set." Amy held her arms in the air as though she'd just scored a goal. She had a pie tin in one hand and a pillowcase in the other.

"What's the pillowcase for?"

Her smile dropped. She stared at him as though he must be delirious. "You need something to put the gold in."

COSMIC CHAOS

Why didn't I think of that? He looked at her sideways as he took the items from her. "At least you're not glitching anymore. That was such a pain."

Amy shot him an angry look. "What's that supposed to mean?"

He shrugged. Apparently there were still issues with her character. Better leave well enough alone. He pushed a button on the wrist remote and looked warily at Amy. "No hanging on this time," he warned.

"Are you kidding me?" Her face lit up with a smile. "I want to see more of what I read about in the Bible. And see more dinosaurs!"

He shook his head. "I'm in a hurry. I won't be coming back here after I've found the gold."

"But—"

"No!" Logan sprinted off, pushing the button on the remote. The backyard grass disappeared as lush, green plants took its place. The aroma of citrus filled his senses—he was definitely back at the same place. *The garden.* He looked around.

No sign of Adam or Eve.

He peeled the black cape from his body. He rolled up the cape and placed it inside the pillowcase, then crept away from the overgrown lemon tree, searching for a river.

The overwhelming smell of fresh sweetness drew

his attention away.

Wait, what is that?

A bush, heavily laden with deep-red strawberries, sat along the trail.

He plucked a succulent berry, nearly the size of his fist, and bit into it.

Juice dribbled down his front, staining his silver uniform.

He used his sleeve to wipe away the wetness still running down his chin. "Mmm, wow." He closed his eyes, savoring the incredible flavor.

The oxygen levels were definitely on full power here.

He breathed in the strength, energy, and vitality, filling every pore of his being. *I wish I could live in this program.*

His eyes popped open.

Why not? Why couldn't I just stay in this program forever? As soon as the thought came, he already had the answer. *Mom. I have to get to her. And to do that, I need to find that gold.* He held the shovel tighter and looked at his surroundings. *How will I find the river?*

Another scent carried on the light breeze.

Vanilla? A memory flashed into his mind of baking cookies with his mom when he was little, breathing in the scent of vanilla as he measured it with the little spoon.

Clusters of fat bananas drooped down in front of him.

His mouth watered.

He shook his head. *C'mon, Logan, focus.*

He pinched his nose with his fingers and shut his eyes tight. He listened.

The distinct song of a chickadee fluttered through the air. And then the trill of a quetzal. Both birds they had studied in an interactive program, but domestic birds were never with tropical birds.

Earlier the program had dinosaurs and man together. It wasn't running correctly. *I hope that doesn't mean I'll be digging up something weird, like pearls instead of gold.* He grunted. *Guess I'll have to find out.*

The trickling of water came from nearby.

He opened his eyes and walked along the path toward the sound.

It grew louder.

He came upon a river. *This must be it!* Heading downstream, he ducked under an almond tree and climbed over plants that looked like broccoli.

Amy had said something about the river flowing from Eden and then dividing into four streams.

He ran alongside the river, dodging fruit trees, exotic flowers, and various vines. Captivating sights and intoxicating smells pulled at his senses, begging him to linger and enjoy. *Not this time.*

He liked how his chest heaved in and out with the intake of air as he ran. His heart pounded within him— a strong beat, keeping tune with the thud of his feet. Even his ribs felt better. But so much running and plant-jumping made him thirsty.

Not one bit tired. Just thirsty.

He knelt down at the water's edge. Cupping his hands, he dipped them in for a drink.

It was unlike any water he'd swallowed before. Clear, sweet, and absolutely refreshing.

They must have figured out a way to amplify taste in this program. Amazing. Logan stood and leaned on the shovel.

The lush garden stopped just ahead. Conifers towered above, while their needles and cones created flat beds below. The river dropped off into a waterfall.

The trek through the forest was easier to manage than the garden, and it didn't take long to reach the cliff's edge.

He crept out.

A small waterfall cascaded to rocks below.

From his vantage point he could clearly see how the river split four ways in the distance. *Bingo. The first one is supposed to be the Pishon.* He followed the lines of the river, determining where it split off first.

The other side.

He'd have to cross over. "Havilah gold, here I come!" With a broad smile, he backed away from the edge. "Aaah!" he cried as he fell—flat on his back, feet in the air.

Overhead, the trees seemed to swirl.

He sat up slowly, eyes closed, allowing his equilibrium to get on track. *What did I trip over?* A fallen tree or stump?

Instead, the intense, yellow eyes of a gray wolf stared back, his hot breath on Logan's face. Logan slowly back-pedaled, careful not to make any sudden moves.

As he crept away, the wolf moved forward, staring with unblinking eyes.

Logan swallowed hard, contemplating those fangs at his throat. He covered his neck with one hand and spun around, heading straight for ... "No!"

The waterfall cliffs loomed beneath him.

Logan's arms flew into the air as he caught his balance. One more step and he would have fallen.

I'm trapped.

Sweat trickled down his neck as he turned to face the wolf.

His hands trembled as the animal stepped closer.

Closer.

The shovel. It was lying there, just a few feet from where he stood. *I can use it to defend myself, but I'll have to be fast.* Logan dove to the ground, rolled, and grabbed the shovel.

Before he could get a good grip, the weight of the wolf slammed into his chest.

"No!" he screamed.

Chapter Eighteen
EMERGENCY MESSAGE

Logan screamed again.

A curious, slobbery sensation covered his face. A wet tongue covered his skin. Licking him. From chin to forehead.

His screams turned to whimpered protests. "It tickles." The whimpering turned to fits of laughter as the wolf's tongue curled behind Logan's ears and up his nose.

The wolf made his way down Logan's uniform,

licking and chewing at the strawberry stains on his chest.

He sat up, laughing as the wolf pressed its nose in harder to get at the berry juice. He rubbed the animal's head, its warm fur soft and luxurious.

The wolf whined in response and resumed licking Logan's face.

"All right, all right." Logan stood up and brushed the conifer needles off his backside. One quick look over the cliff confirmed it was too steep to manage hiking. "How am I gonna get down there?"

As if in response to Logan's question, the wolf took off running along the cliff's edge. He stopped at a moss-covered boulder and stared at Logan.

"You want me to follow?"

Animals never behaved this way in interactive programs. But then, Nanny's programs weren't normal, either.

The wolf gave him a calculating stare with its head low.

"Well, I guess I can't expect you to talk to me, can I?" He reached down and grabbed the shovel and pillowcase.

As soon as he started walking, the wolf took off running again, somewhere below the edge.

When Logan reached the boulder, he discovered a

footpath zigzagging to the bottom, but he never could catch a glimpse of the wolf again. He hiked down a ways before coming to a narrow place in the river. A little farther he came to a sandy, beach-like area next to the Pishon. He lifted the shovel and started digging, on high alert for the sparkle of gold.

The sand gave way to dark, rich earth. Soft and easy to push the shovel into.

He worked at it, digging and searching along the river for what seemed like hours. Logan stopped to scratch at an itch on his scalp. But it was useless trying, with that annoying helmet in the way. He threw the shovel down and tugged. His neck bones popped and cracked as he jerked to get the helmet free.

It didn't budge.

I'll just have to ignore it. He picked up the shovel and went back to work.

The niggling, squirming, itching of his scalp grew worse.

This time, he grabbed a stick and worked it into a small opening. Then he pried the cold, blue egg from his head like a suction cup.

Pop!

His fingernails scratched away at the dry skin.

Wait a minute. Where are the blisters? He pressed his fingers across his smooth scalp, front to back, then side to side. *How'd it heal so fast?*

The helmet lay on the sand in front of him.

Maybe it worked better than the nurses thought it would.

He kept digging. That gold was around here somewhere.

Something behind him moved.

He turned.

A herd of animals made their way toward the river. Some walked on hind legs, making them as tall as sixteen feet high. Their long tails bobbed behind them.

Iguanodons.

So graceful and swift as they congregated to the water.

Something bumped him.

One of these amazing animals, a much smaller one, rubbed its head against Logan's arm.

Startled, he stepped back.

It came at him, nuzzling into his neck.

Logan lifted his hand and touched the smooth, leather-like skin.

The Iguanodon responded like an affectionate house cat, nearly knocking Logan over.

He laughed out loud.

An odd sound came from one of the animals at the river.

Logan's new friend popped up its head, as though

listening to a mother's call, then hurried off to meet her.

It all seems so real. He examined the sky. The sun was much lower than it should be. "It's that late already?" Gripping the handle of the shovel, he winced. His palms were really sore.

Red, raw skin.

"Man, that hurts." He grabbed the pillowcase and ripped pieces from the top. After wrapping each hand, he looked like a boxer. But at least he could still dig.

He plunged the shovel in again ... and hit something. Logan's heart skipped.

A red light on his wrist remote flashed.

Nanny's voice came from it. "Logan, I'm ending the program now."

"What? No, not now!"

"You have an emergency message from your father. Something's wrong."

Chapter Nineteen
STOLEN

Logan felt the change, more than saw it. His lungs went from being light and airy to heavy and constrained. His head throbbed.

As soon as the sky apartment came into full view, he turned to the hologram.

"Logan," his dad said with urgency, "an emergency news broadcast came through ten minutes ago. All the newly improved Nanny Express Five Thousands are being recalled."

"What? But I'm just starting to—" Logan stopped. He shouldn't share with his dad what he's been up to. *No point in getting Dad's hopes up about the gold.*

His dad held his hands up. "Son, you don't understand. This is *serious*. An experimental time travel chip was stolen from the University of Tech Science. They believe the chip was hidden in one of the new Nanny models."

Time travel chip? He looked at Nanny. It was all real? Without a doubt, she had the chip imbedded in her.

Whoa.

"Did you hear what I said?" His dad interrupted Logan's thoughts. "I'm sending a transport to come get her right now. Make sure she's in the box and ready to go. She's too dangerous to keep."

His insides sank. "Sure, Dad." What else could Logan say?

"This is actually good timing. That purchase will get credited back to my account. And we can definitely use the money right now. It might be enough to get at least one of us out of here." He winked and the hologram flashed off.

I need that gold to get us both back to Mom. I just need more time with Nanny! Logan looked around the sky apartment. He had to think fast.

His gaze settled on the crate that Nanny had arrived in. *That's it!*

"Nanny, I need your help." *Where is she?*

A cold hand reached around his neck from behind. "You aren't getting rid of me." Her voice seethed with anger.

"No, I'm not getting rid of you, I promise." Logan started to swallow, but couldn't. He tried to pull her fingers off. "I have a plan, but I need your help. Please."

She squeezed tighter.

At this rate he would be dead in a few minutes.

"Wait, Mommy," his strangled voice cried out. "Mommy! Stop!"

Nanny released him, spun him around, and came nearly nose to nose with him. "You still want me to be your mommy?" Her high-pitched voice sounded meek and hopeful.

He coughed, trying to catch his breath. "Yes, yes. You aren't going anywhere." He tried to keep his voice soothing. "But to keep you here, to keep you as my mommy, I need your help."

"Certainly, Logan," she gushed, embracing him. "Anything."

He pulled back from her suffocating arms and pointed to his room. "Grab Maggie and put her in the box you came in. When the transport arrives, you need to hide. Don't say or do *anything* until they leave."

Nanny raised a finely manicured eyebrow and smiled. "You are a clever boy." She did exactly as he instructed.

Within the hour, the door beeped.

"Transport here," a voice said.

"Enter," Logan replied.

An enormous robot ducked down through the doorway. Rusted bolts, much larger than they should be, seemed to hold him together.

126

COSMIC CHAOS

"Is this ready to go?" The way his jaw wagged when he talked didn't match up to his words. He pointed to the crate Nanny had arrived in.

Logan nodded. He bit his lip, hoping his plan would work.

The giant robot patted the container with massive hands. He lifted the box and hoisted it over his shoulder. Without another word, he left the sky apartment.

Logan released his breath. "You can come out now, Nanny."

Nanny poked her head out from his room, then approached him. "Your plan worked." She squeezed his shoulder, and it wasn't even painful. "I'll have dinner ready for you soon."

His stomach rumbled with the mention of food. "Dinner can wait. I need to get back to the Pishon." He started to press a button on his wrist remote, then stopped. His shovel had hit something when he had to leave in a hurry. *How do I return to that exact moment?* His headache pounded, making it harder to think.

Nanny had tracked his travel patterns in reverse to get Amy home. *Will that work now? Can't hurt to try.* He punched the buttons on the remote, then stopped when the reality of the situation came crashing down on him.

Time travel.

He blinked. *Eden is a real place? And Amy isn't an interactive character. She's real. No wonder she didn't act like she was supposed to. And I've treated her badly. I've been horrible, just like she said.* Logan swallowed hard.

I can't go back. Ever.

All the excitement and eagerness from moments ago vanished.

As he processed his thoughts, a glimmer of hope took hold. *I don't need Amy, I can go directly to the Pishon River.*

But just as quickly as the thought came, his teacher's voice from last year, hammering one fact into the students, filled Logan's mind. *"If time travel were ever possible, it would be too dangerous to use. We can't risk altering history. Any small change could drastically affect humankind."*

It felt like a meteor had sunk into his belly, growing heavier by the minute. *How much history have I changed already? And was it for better or worse?*

"Logan." Nanny came closer. She put her hand on top of his head. "My sensors indicate something is wrong. Are you feeling all right?"

He shook his head. *Everything is wrong.*

She picked Logan up, gently cradling his thin body in her arms. "There, there, now. Mommy is here." She laid him in his bed.

COSMIC CHAOS

Hopelessness enveloped him like the blanket Nanny covered him with. *I'll go to school tomorrow, and they'll force the implant in me. And then I'll die a slow and miserable death. And I'll never see Mom again.* Tears streamed from his eyes. He didn't wipe them away. Why bother?

Chapter Twenty
UNEXPECTED GUEST

Logan woke to a beeping noise. He rubbed the crusties from his eyes. His nose felt plugged from so much crying earlier. *Ugh. I'm such a baby.* He sat up.

A headache slammed into his skull.

He immediately slunk down.

Thoughts about his situation tumbled in his mind.

I don't want to die from a chip implant. He sat up slowly, carefully cradling his head. "Lights. Dim."

The light turned on in his bedroom, set at dim, just as he requested. It still seemed too bright.

He fumbled around in his toolbox until he pulled out the card from his mom. *What do I do, Mom? I can't stay up here. I need you.*

The fresh scent of lemon came from the open drawer.

The urgency of his situation overtook his thoughts. *I'm coming, Mom. I'll find the gold in the Pishon River. And I'll do it without disrupting history. You can count on it.* He gazed at the card with fondness.

COSMIC CHAOS

Something beeped again. *A hologram? This late?* He suddenly came fully awake. *Mom!*

Logan left his room and scurried through the darkness. "Receive." His voice sounded hoarse.

"Logan." His dad's face appeared before him. Instead of being at the office, it looked like he was in some sort of public transport shuttle.

Logan tried to brush aside the disappointment.

Dark circles rimmed his dad's eyes and his face sagged. "I can't sleep. I can't think." He groaned, while rubbing the back of his neck. "There's just—" He stopped talking and took a good look at Logan. He blinked his eyes. "What's on your head, son?"

Logan touched the fuzz on his head. "Oh, it's just ... well, I ..." *What was that? And why did Dad notice this but not the water-soaked uniform?*

His dad lifted his hand and pressed it into the air. "Don't bother. You can tell me when I get there."

"What do you mean, 'get there'?"

"I'm taking time off work. The demands for this new oxygen system are just too intense. I'm not left with any time to make plans for ..." He lowered his voice as he leaned forward. "I'm coming home."

Logan stared at him in disbelief. "You mean, you're coming *here*?"

His dad nodded, as though it were a normal,

131

everyday occurrence.

"Okay." Logan didn't know what else to say. The last time his dad set foot in the sky apartment was five years ago when he had helped Logan move in.

"I'm glad you answered the hologram. I didn't want to surprise you by arriving in the middle of the night." He gave a heavy sigh. "After all these years, they still haven't finished the tunnel between biodomes, so I'm using the underground transport system. *Six hours* of congested traffic, even at this time of night." He shook his head in disbelief. "I'm getting close, though. I'll be there soon."

The hologram clicked off.

Logan looked around the tiny apartment. *Where's he gonna sleep?* He looked at the space between the hologram projector and the small kitchen table. *I wonder how tall he is.* He pushed the table against the wall to make more space. His dad would be there soon.

"Would you like breakfast, Logan?" Nanny came out of the shadows, her voice quiet and pensive.

His head jerked up. "Oh, no! I can't let Dad see you." He ran toward her. "I have to hide you, fast."

"I can hide in your room again."

"No. That won't work." He sat hard on the chair. "What if he comes into my room for some reason?" He pressed his palm into his forehead.

COSMIC CHAOS

The wrist remote slid down his arm.

He sat up straight. "I'll hide you at Amy's house. There's a shed in her backyard."

Nanny gave him a hard look. Her unblinking eyes stared uncomfortably long.

"I'll come get you as soon as Dad leaves, I promise."

"It's my job to take care of you."

"I'll have my wrist remote on. You can talk to me *anytime*."

"You won't get rid of me that easily." She lunged forward, reaching out to grab him.

Logan sidestepped, avoiding her grasp. He spun around and climbed underneath the table for protection. His head ached from the quick movements, and his lungs seemed to be filled with lead.

A pod docked out front, the connection tubes hissing, and Logan's heart hammered in his chest. "He's here! I have to get you out *now*."

Nanny flung the table across the room, shattering it.

Logan's mind raced as he scrambled to find safety. *What had Troy said?* "Nanny," Logan ordered, "stand by!"

Chapter Twenty-One
HIDING PLACE

Nanny's eyes closed as her chin dropped to her chest.

"It worked. It really worked." Relief cascaded over him. Logan punched numbers into the wrist remote to get to Amy's about the same time as before.

He wrapped his arms around Nanny.

From the other side of the apartment door, his dad started using voice activation to unlock it.

Everything faded out.

Amy's house came into view.

Logan let go of Nanny's stiff body, allowing her to fall to the ground.

Amy sat on the back step, reading the Bible in her lap as a gentle breeze stirred her hair.

He took a deep breath, the rich air sinking into his lungs and melting away his headache. He walked toward Amy.

She looked up, startled. "Oh! The way you appear like that is so creepy, but I guess I'm going to have to get used to it." Her jaw went slack, and she leaned forward. "What happened to you?"

Logan's eyebrows scrunched together. "What do you mean?"

"Well, last time you were here you were like plastic surgery gone bad." She paused for emphasis. "Really bad." She stared hard at him. "And now …"

"Now what?"

"You look different. For one thing, you have hair. And your skin is golden, like you've been to the tropics on vacation."

He *had* been in the tropics, sort of. At least that's what the garden felt like. And it was real. Which meant … dinosaurs and man existed at the same time? He scratched his head.

"So where's the gold?" She looked at him expectantly.

He gazed into the sky, heaving a great sigh. "Come with me." He had more important things to deal with right now.

Amy followed him to the fence where Nanny was. "Why did you bring your mom?" She slapped a hand over her mouth. "Sorry. You don't like questions."

Logan gave a sheepish grin. "No, it's okay. You can ask me questions." He couldn't look her in the eyes. "I didn't know … well, I thought you were …" *Why do apologies have to be so hard?* He tried again. "I'm sorry I've

135

been so mean."

A smile curved up the side of her mouth. "Well, it's not like I've been the nicest person, either. Start over?" She held her hand out for a shake.

Logan gripped her hand. The apology wasn't as hard as he thought it would be. Maybe Amy wasn't so bad after all.

Amy's eyes filled with concern as she stared at Nanny. "What's wrong with her? Is she hurt?"

"No." Logan grunted as he pushed her into an upright position. "I'm going to hide her here for a while." He caught himself speaking in a demanding voice, like before. "Um, if that's okay with you."

Amy looked at Logan, suspicion etched on her face. "Is she a fugitive or something?"

"No, she's just ..." He looked directly at her. "She's the time machine."

Amy gasped. "You mean, she's not real?" She rubbed her fingers over the soft, life-like skin of Nanny. "Amazing."

"Just a robot." He'd lost his fascination with Nanny once she'd started hurting him.

"I knew you were a time traveler," Amy gushed. "I can't wait to tell Bekah!"

"Hold on, you can't tell *anyone*. Altering history is always a risk, so the fewer people that know about me, the better."

Amy shrugged, then looked at Nanny again. "Well, I suppose you could hide her in the shed." Amy chewed on her painted fingernails. "Although, if my parents see her in there, they'll think she's a real person."

"We can cover her up. She won't be here long." Right? After all, his dad wouldn't be staying long at the apartment, would he? Logan readjusted his grip on Nanny. "Let's get her in there."

Amy nodded and headed toward the toolshed.

They positioned Nanny in the corner of the shed and covered her.

"If anybody lifts that tarp," Amy said, "they're gonna be totally freaked out." She grinned. "And I'd love to see the look on their faces."

Chapter Twenty-Two
DEACTIVATED

"Nanny's on standby mode," Logan explained to Amy. "I've got to get home. My dad is waiting for me."

"But how can you time travel when she's turned off?"

"Remember the wrist remote? I can still access her that way, even when she's on standby. I just figured that out when I brought her here." He lifted his hand in a wave. "'Bye." Logan took in one long, deep breath, holding it in like sweet dessert in his mouth. Then he pressed the button on his wrist remote to return home.

"There you are," his dad said, coming out of the viral chamber.

Logan put his arms out to get his balance as he struggled to suck air in.

"You okay, son?" His dad put an oxygen mask on Logan's face.

The air came in easier, and his lungs started to relax.

"Wow, you've grown." His dad stared at Logan as though seeing him for the first time. "You look different in person than on the hologram." His head tilted. "You've got more color to your face."

Logan looked away and nodded. He added quietly, "Last time we saw each other I was just seven years old."

"Yeah, well." His dad looked around, an uncomfortable silence between them. "My office is bigger than your apartment." He loomed like a giant in the small space. As he unbuckled the safety harness from his chest and legs, his bulky muscles flexed within his silver uniform. His moon boots were more rugged, likely for rappelling down oxygen tubes.

"I thought you just worked in the office, Dad."

His dad nodded. "Most of the time. But once in a while I have to get out there myself and show them how to connect the new custom oxygen conductors." His voice sounded weary.

Even in the dim light, Logan could tell some of his dad's black eyebrow hairs had turned gray. And there were more crease lines—especially around his eyes and forehead.

His dad stopped when he neared the broken table Nanny had splintered.

"A bit of an accident. I'll get it cleaned up." Logan stood, the mask still over his mouth.

"No, no. It can wait until morning. We need to get

to sleep."

It was obvious his dad wasn't going to fit where the tiny table had been. The closet-sized kitchen was no good, either. "Do you want to take my bed, Dad? I can just sleep out here."

His dad sighed. "Yeah, that's a great idea. Don't wake me in the morning. I'll hang out here while you're at school."

"Sure."

His dad had to turn to fit his broad shoulders through the tiny doorframe of Logan's bedroom.

As soon as the door shut, Logan took another long suck from the oxygen mask.

Back to the Pishon River.

He stopped for a moment. It was midnight here. But it was afternoon at Amy's. And late afternoon at the Pishon, getting close to twilight. *How do I know what time I'll arrive?*

The backtracking option on the wrist remote would return him to the same time he had left.

I'll have to dig in the dark. He grabbed a light pulsar from the kitchen cabinet. *I can't wait to see the look on Dad's face when he sees the pile of gold I bring him.*

COSMIC CHAOS

It didn't take long for Logan to get the light pulsar set up so he could see in the darkness. It actually wasn't too bad. The light from the moon and stars was so bright he probably could have done just fine without the pulsar.

The shovel was where he left it. He picked it up, hands cramping. He pushed the tip into the soft earth, feeling around with it until he hit the spot he'd hoped for.

There!

He pushed the shovel deep to the side of the object and brought it to the surface. He fell to his knees, body trembling, and brushed away the dark soil to reveal ... a big rock.

All this work, all this time, all for nothing.

I need a map or something to show me the layout of the land. His body wasn't used to this physical labor. Every muscle ached. But his hands didn't hurt anymore. He pulled off the cloth and looked at them.

No raw skin. No blisters. Nothing. Just his palms, completely healed.

Then there had been his blistered head. After hours here, both injuries healed. He felt his forehead where the lump had been.

Just a little swelling left.

This place is amazing. I wonder what else the Bible says

about it.

Maybe there was a map in the Bible.

He'd go ask Amy. *But first, I need sleep and food.* He lifted his hand to press the buttons on his remote to get home.

The lights were flashing in odd ways.

"Huh?" He pressed a button and found himself ...

"Logan!" Amy shrieked his name as soon as she came into view. "You've got to do something. Ben is missing!"

Logan froze. *How did Amy manage to get me here? Maybe she isn't what she seems.* He stared hard at her. *Could she be a spy from the One World Galaxy Foundation?*

"Hello? Are you listening to me?" She shook Logan's arm. "Ben loves anything robotic or remote-controlled." Her words came out rushed. "He must have found Nanny and figured out how to time travel even though she's turned off!"

"That's impossible."

"I'm supposed to be watching him while my parents are gone. They'll be home any minute, and I need to find him!"

"Okay, okay. I just don't think he's time traveled. He's probably just around here somewhere." He scanned the backyard.

"I've looked everywhere. He is *not* here. What am I

supposed to do? Sit here and argue with you about the improbability of this happening? Do something!"

Logan looked at Nanny. She still wasn't awake.

Could Ben really have figured out a way to access her time travel capabilities while she slept? Or did she wake up, send him somewhere, then go on standby mode again?

Logan found the tracking button on his wrist remote and pressed it.

A green light blipped across the small screen.

"Someone has accessed this program for ..."

"What? What is it?"

"The garden of Eden." He examined the screen. "See, this shows my recent activity. This green light shows another person is in the program." He paused. "I mean, it shows someone else time traveling."

"He probably doesn't even know how to get home. He might be scared or hurt, or ..." Amy's voice quavered.

"Worse yet, he could alter history in drastic ways. We've got to get him out of there. Come on!"

She grabbed hold of Logan's arm and squeezed her eyes shut. "I'm ready."

He pressed the button.

Soon, the luscious scent of fresh lemons surrounded them.

Amy let go of his arm. "Where do we look?"

"I don't know. If he started here, what do you think he would have been drawn to?"

She gasped.

A fiery sword stood in midair. It glowed white-hot and cut through the air in swift circles, making its way around a tree.

Logan tensed. "Is that the same tree that had the snake?"

"No." She stared with her mouth wide open. "That was different—the Tree of the Knowledge of Good and Evil. This must be the Tree of Life. Which means—"

"What? Means what?"

"We have to get out of here. Now!" She took off running.

"Could you at least explain to me—?"

Something moved in the corner of his vision ... the fiery sword.

And it was flying through the air, headed straight for them.

Chapter Twenty-Three
THE SWORD

Logan followed Amy, the sword a few hundred feet behind, coming at them.

He nearly toppled over Amy as she skidded to a stop.

A seven-foot warrior blocked the path ahead. He stood with his back to them, glistening-white, sparkling, and shimmering. His feet didn't quite touch the ground. Instead, he hovered over it. Plus, Logan could see the path through the figure.

"That's weird," said Logan. "He doesn't look real. I thought this wasn't a simulation."

"He's real enough," Amy said. "He's an angel, blocking Adam and Eve from entering the garden."

"Why? What happened?"

"I can't explain now. We've got to get out of here. I just wish I knew if Ben was already out."

The angel made eye contact. He looked ready to pound them.

They bolted off the path and scrambled over

lavender bushes, shaking the scent into the air. They trampled zinnia blooms and ducked under sugar snap peas.

Amy dove under fig tree branches.

The warrior's footsteps were fast approaching.

Logan made his escape right behind Amy.

She stumbled and rolled. "Aaah!"

They found themselves in the same field they'd been in before when they had followed Adam and come across the deer.

Amy grabbed at her ankle and sucked air in. "It hurts," she said, trying to sound brave but not doing a good job.

"Go! He's still coming after us!" He grabbed hold of her arm and flung it across his shoulders, then wrapped his other arm around her waist and pulled her along.

"Stop, Logan!"

He stopped and looked back.

The warrior stood at the border of the garden, muscular arms crossed and legs spread, a firm expression on his face.

"He won't come after us here." Her hand covered her ankle.

"Are you sure?"

"Yeah. He's assigned to protect the garden."

"He wasn't there last time we were here."

"Logan," she whimpered, in tears now, "you need to take me home. I think it's broken."

"What about your brother?"

"I can't do anything in this condition." Her shoulders drooped. "Please, Logan. It hurts so much." Tears rolled down her cheeks. "I have to find Ben, but how can I search for him like this?"

"We can't risk him staying here any longer. He might change the course of history. Do you have any idea what that means?"

Amy's crying turned to sobs.

"It can't be that bad. Let me have a look."

She lifted her hand.

Dark-red blood trickled from her skin where the bone punched through.

Logan jerked back and looked away. "All right. I guess you really do need medical treatment."

She sniffled and wiped her eyes with the back of her sleeve.

He stood, examining the wrist remote. He paused before pushing the buttons. "The moon has faster treatment." He nodded to himself. "And the faster you're treated, the sooner we can return to find Ben."

"But wouldn't they want my insurance papers and try to notify my parents?"

"No, they'd just scan you and—" He hung his head

for a moment. "I suppose that could be a problem. Unless—"

"Shh!" Amy put her fingers to her mouth. "Did you hear that?"

A faint crying came from behind the bushes.

"It could be Ben. Go see," she pleaded.

"Are you sure?" Logan gave her ankle a wary look.

"Just go!"

Logan walked toward the crying. Leaving Amy alone when she was in pain felt wrong, but the warrior seemed intent on staying put, so things seemed safe enough.

Amy's voice carried on the breeze. "Dear God, help me!"

He swallowed hard. He needed to get Ben fast. *The little moonworm*. Logan ran, stopping only a few times to reassess where the sound came from.

Deep, racking wails came from someone ... definitely an adult, not a kid.

And the person cried as if someone had died.

If Ben is dead, this could be bad. Really bad. Finally at the edge of the field, Logan came to a grove of trees and stopped. He bent over, allowing the fresh oxygen to fill his galloping lungs.

A long, wide branch touched down from a tree trunk to the ground, then into the air again. There, a man and woman held each other.

Adam and Eve.

But they wore clothes this time ... some kind of animal furs. Eve wailed and sobbed. Adam's face scrunched up as tears streamed from his eyes. They rocked back and forth in their sorrow.

There was no sign of Ben.

Logan inched away quietly, not wanting to intrude on their private grief. He walked back toward Amy.

What he saw in the field nearly made his heart stop.

The warrior had left the garden entrance and stood over Amy, a sword drawn.

Something welled up inside him. A strength he'd never felt before.

Courage.

Logan ran to save his friend.

The angel, bright as lightning, lifted his sword high, as if to strike.

The sword came down right on top of Amy.

Chapter Twenty-Four
TROUBLE

"Noooooo!" he shouted.

The warrior looked his way, just as Logan took a flying leap to tackle him.

Logan braced himself, expecting to hit a brick wall. Instead, he felt air, then the thud of hard ground. He rolled to his feet, then searched for his opponent.

The warrior had disappeared. Vanished.

"Logan!" Amy cried. "Logan!"

He swiveled around to find her, help her in her dying moments. His heart hurt, ached in those few seconds.

Her face shone, glowing with happiness. A broad smile poured out laughter.

"Are you dead? Am I seeing a ghost?"

"No." She stood up and embraced him.

He stayed stiff as a board.

"I asked God for help," she said, "and He sent over the angel."

"Angel? You mean that beast that attacked you?"

"No, Logan. He put his sword into my wound. Look ... look what happened!"

Logan bent down to examine her ankle.

She rolled her foot in a circle. No punctures, no exposed bone, no fresh blood. "It ... it looks fine." He stared up at her.

"I've never had an answer to prayer like that before. It was awesome!"

Adrenaline coursed through his body, and he shook, still trying to make sense of what just happened. "So, you're okay?"

She smiled again. Her face held such peace. She nodded. "I'm better than okay." She tugged his arm and headed in Adam and Eve's direction.

Logan felt his insides settling. A little. "Not that way. That's not Ben that's crying."

"Then who—" A knowing look came over her face, and she slowly nodded.

He watched her. How could she know anything without seeing?

She pointed to his wrist remote. "Can you see where we are in relation to Ben?"

He lifted the remote and pressed a button to calculate the coordinates. "Look at this."

Amy leaned in close, watching the green dot blip across the screen, while the red dot stayed in position.

"He's not that far from us."

"I just wonder where he thinks he's going. C'mon."

They crossed through the field into tropical, leafy vegetation, which slowed them down. Tall palms provided shelter for what sounded like thousands of birds. Brightly colored parrots swept over their heads, chasing after enormous flying insects. The abundant ferns in various sizes were easy enough to get through, but the clusters of green horse-tail plants walled them off from going any farther.

"What now?" Amy asked. "We need a machete to get through this stuff."

To the side, short trees topped with long, skinny leaves spiraled out from thick, diamond-patterned trunks. They partially hid gray boulders that appeared to be scattered like a game of giant marbles.

"Look." He pointed. "If we climb across the boulders, it won't take us too far off course."

Amy paused, studying their location. "Do you really think Ben went through here?"

Logan sighed. "How do I know?" He checked his wrist remote. "He may have gone a roundabout way, but we'll get to him faster if we cut through." He jumped onto a small boulder.

Something blocked the sunlight for a moment, and they both looked up.

COSMIC CHAOS

Logan shielded his eyes from the bright rays. "What is that?"

Whatever it was, it began to circle overhead.

Amy's jaw fell open. "Is that an eagle?" Her voice held a measure of awe, and she examined the bird as it glided through the air. "Look how big it is—aaaaah!"

Amy's high-pitched scream sent chills down Logan's back. He spun around, expecting to see her being carried off by a bird. Instead, a huge mosquito, the size of a jumbo-sized crayon, perched on her upper arm. It was drawing blood from her like sucking a milkshake from a straw.

"Smash it!" Logan yelled.

Her voice quavered. "I … can't." Amy's horrified face turned white.

Logan jumped from his rock and smashed the mosquito with his palm. Blood and guts splattered all over him and Amy.

"Ewwwww!" She bobbed up and down, completely grossed out. The punctured area continued to bleed as the toxins injected into her made her arm swell.

Logan pulled a long leaf from a nearby tree and wrapped it around her arm to stop the bleeding. "I just hope this isn't poisonous."

"What, the leaf?"

"Yeah."

She jerked her arm away. "It better not be. My arm already itches bad enough."

"Let's just hope that massive mosquito wasn't carrying any massive viruses."

"So disgusting." Amy sounded like she was about to cry. Instead, she sat down hard and buried her head against her knees.

"Are you okay?"

She didn't answer.

With the amount of toxins just loaded into her body, she could get a fever.

"Yeah," she finally responded with a terse voice. "Just fine. Let's go."

Logan re-climbed the first boulder, then onto the second, looking back to make certain Amy was following. He watched her carefully for any signs of illness.

"Are we getting any closer?"

Logan checked the wrist remote. "He's headed in that direction." He pointed north. "And he's moving fast. Like he's running."

Amy gasped. "He must be in trouble."

Once past the boulders, the vegetation thinned and the kids ran, avoiding anything that looked like it might slow them down. They finally came to a rise, and when they reached the top, they looked below.

COSMIC CHAOS

"There's Ben." Logan pointed to a small figure in the distance. "Let's go."

"Finally!" Amy went ahead of him, carefully traversing the steep, muddy terrain. "Ben!" she yelled.

Logan let her sprint ahead as he slowed. He needed to get back to digging for gold.

The grassy plains stretched for miles before them, similar to what Logan had seen in an African safari program.

"Ben!" Amy yelled again, still running.

Ben turned his head and looked back, nearly stumbling.

"Amy, look," he shouted, chest heaving. He pointed to a group of large birds, similar to ostriches, but without feathers.

"Naked ostriches! Aren't they funny looking?"

Amy scolded her brother, yelling something about scaring the wits out of her. She hugged him hard.

"Now we can finally get out of here," Logan grumbled.

Amy walked to Logan, an arm tight around Ben. "Don't ever, ever do anything like this again. I've been worried sick over you."

"I know," Ben whined. "You don't have to keep saying it." He looked over his shoulder. "I wanted to touch one, but they were too fast."

"We've gotta get out of here," Logan ordered. "Both of you put a hand on me."

"But I don't want to go." Ben backed away. "I want to see more dinosaurs!"

Logan grabbed his shoulder and jerked him closer.

"Cut it out," Amy said, "you'll hurt him!"

"Uuuugh." Logan put a hand over his mouth. "What is that *smell*?"

"Oh," Ben snickered. "I found a fresh, hot dung pile from a triceratops." His eyes grew wide with wonder. He waved his hands in the air as he spoke. "There were these massive black beetles swarming all over it." He reached into his pocket and pulled out a smashed, black carcass. "See? I was trying to get a good look at them burrowing holes, and I got a little poopy in the process." His grin was a proud one.

"Ewww, that's gross!" Amy held her hands in the air as if they were contaminated. "I'm not touching you."

"Just put a finger on me," Logan said wearily. "We need to get you both home."

A dark shadow fell over them.

He looked up.

A large, lizard-like animal loomed over them with razor teeth, its open mouth ready to chomp and chew.

A T-Rex!

Amy's scream could have split hairs.

COSMIC CHAOS

Chapter Twenty-Five
CO-CONSPIRATOR

Logan grabbed Ben's shirt, fell on Amy, and pressed the button on the remote as all three of them screamed.

They opened their eyes to find themselves in Amy's toolshed.

"Whoa, we almost got ate for lunch. Totally awesome!" Ben jumped up from the concrete floor and poised his hand for a high-five from anyone who was willing.

Both Logan and Amy released a deep sigh and lay on the cold floor.

"Nearly getting *eaten* by a T-Rex is far from awesome," Amy chastised Ben. She sat up, arms crossed. "Ben, the toolshed is off limits to you. Do you hear me?"

Logan sat up and stared at Nanny.

She wasn't covered by the tarp anymore.

"Ben, how did you do it?"

Ben shifted his weight to the other foot, shrugging his shoulders. "Well, I just came in here looking for

Amy." He looked sideways at her. "I really wanted you to make me a peanut-butter-and-jelly sandwich."

Amy rolled her eyes.

At the mention of food, Logan's stomach growled. *When was the last time I ate?*

Ben pointed at Nanny. "When I came in here, I saw that lady."

"And …?" Logan motioned with his hand, encouraging Ben to continue.

"Well, she has that red light blinking on her," he said, as if that was all the explanation that was needed.

Logan turned to look at Nanny.

Sure enough, a faint, red light was blinking near her collarbone.

He turned to Ben. "And …?"

"I wanted to know how it got inside her skin. But when I asked, she wouldn't answer me. I shook her hard, but she just kept sleeping. So, I pushed at the red light, and a little door opened."

Amy shot him a surprised look.

"Here," Ben said, "I'll show you." Ben pushed against Nanny's skin.

A panel opened, revealing more blinking lights and circuit boards. "She's like the Bionic Woman in my comic books. Then …" He stood on his tiptoes, hands in the air. "See that red microchip in there? It doesn't look right—you know, like it doesn't match the other components. So I tried to jiggle it out."

"You what?" Both Amy and Logan spoke the words at the same time.

"She didn't wake up or say anything. And then, all of a sudden, I was somewhere else and saw some really cool animals. Until you came and got me. How did you do that, anyway?"

"All right." Logan pressed his hand against his forehead. "Don't come in this shed anymore. You could have really messed up history, big time."

"History? What do you mean?"

"Ben, you need to take a shower," Amy said. "I'll explain later."

"Wait, Amy, I ..." Logan needed to ask for her help, but why would she give it to him after the way he'd treated Ben? "I really need to look at your mom's Bible and see if there are any maps."

"Yeah, there are maps in the back." She shrugged. "Mostly of the Holy Land."

"I'm looking for something specific. Anything about Havilah and the Pishon River." He looked away. "I couldn't find the gold." He grew lightheaded.

She turned to her brother. "Ben, go inside." Amy fixed her eyes on Logan. "All right, Logan, if you want my help, you need to explain to me what exactly you're doing." She used a firm tone, but not a harsh one. "I know you don't want to, but if you tell me what your goal is, I won't have to keep wondering if the information I'm giving you is helpful."

"I wanna help too," Ben said.

"Ben!"

"Okay," Ben grumbled. "I'm going inside."

"Make sure he doesn't come back in here." Logan grabbed for the wall to keep himself steady as the room tilted. His breathing quickened. Sweat beaded on his forehead.

"Yeah, well, I don't know if keeping the time machine here is such a great idea. There's no way I can keep him out."

Logan *thunk*ed to the floor and blacked out.

Logan's eyes opened slowly. He was lying on Amy's green couch, facing the dining area and open kitchen. Amy sat at a chair next to him, reading. Logan tried to sit up.

Amy jumped up. "Hey, you okay?" she asked. "You got really pale, then passed out." She knelt beside him.

He buried his face in his hands. "I'm just worn out." His dry mouth made his voice sound raspy. "And thirsty." Just then, his stomach cramped for food.

"And hungry."

"I thought you might be hungry. I put together a sandwich for you."

Ben walked into the kitchen, freshly showered.

"Ben." She pointed to the counter. "Grab that sandwich for Logan. And get him some water too."

Ben walked over with the food and a glass of water.

Logan balanced the plate on his knees and lifted the sandwich, staring at it for a moment. The mixed scents of creamy nuttiness with the sweet fruit was irresistible. He shoved it into his mouth and bit down. A brief smile was soon replaced with a frown as the peanut butter stuck to the roof of his mouth. He opened his mouth and used his tongue to pry it loose.

Amy smirked. "What's the matter? They don't have PB & Js where you come from?"

Logan talked with his mouth full. "Not exactly, no."

Ben's eyes went wide with unbelief. "How can you live without peanut-butter-and-jelly sandwiches? What do you eat?"

Logan worked his tongue to get the last of the sticky stuff loose before he answered. "A powder mixed with synthetic water. It has vitamins and minerals, as well as chemicals, to kill any bacteria, diseases, and viruses."

"You eat chemicals?" Ben looked shocked. "Do you have cancer?"

COSMIC CHAOS

"Is that why you didn't have hair when you first came?" Amy asked.

Logan was too hungry and tired to answer their dumb questions. So he just kept chewing.

Amy shook her head.

He sat forward, looking intently at Amy. "I have a question for *you* first." He swallowed. "I want to know how you brought me here from the Pishon River to help you find Ben." His voice came out edgy. "What are you not telling me?"

"I ... well." Her head tilted as though considering how to say it. "I know I wasn't supposed to touch Nanny. And I'm sorry!" She put her hands up in mock surrender. "But I was searching everywhere for Ben, and when I went into the toolshed, she was lying there uncovered. The panel was open and ... and the little, red chip looked like it had fallen to the floor, so I put it back in. Then you showed up. I didn't know that replacing the chip would bring you back here."

Her story sounded legit. *But so much of my time has been wasted because of Ben.* He needed to get out of here. He guzzled the water, tasting the gentle sweetness as it refreshed him.

"Ben, help me get things cleaned up. Mom and Dad will be back soon from the homeschool convention."

"I'm going now. I need to check on my dad." *Is he*

still sleeping? Making plans for our escape?

Logan stood, gave a slight wave, then pushed the button on his remote.

The sky apartment came into view. His dad sat there, hunched over, working with something on his lap. The kid-sized chair looked as though it would break under his dad's weight at any moment.

"Dad?" He sucked in the air slowly, concentrating on keeping his lungs filled, rubbing his arms against the chill.

His dad looked up. "Logan?" he looked puzzled. "You're not at school?" His focus returned to the flat type pad in his lap.

"I ..." He tried to act normal with his dad. "I'm not going back."

His dad's head swung up fast as he sat straight and leaned forward. "What did you say?" he asked, as if Logan has just threatened him.

Logan forced his voice to sound firm. "I'm not going back to school."

His dad set the type pad aside. "And why not?" The question sounded like a challenge. The muscles in his jaw tightened.

Logan swallowed hard, working to sound confident, even though he didn't feel it. He held up his arm. "No chip implant."

COSMIC CHAOS

His dad lifted a hand in the air as if to say, *So what?*

"Starting today, they're required for every student."

His dad pointed a finger at him. "Not for you. You are a medical exception."

"Not anymore. If I go to school, the implants are required, no matter what."

His dad looked down for a moment, then breathed in deep, raking his fingers over his bald head. "I guess there's no point in fighting it. Lockdown is in two days, and I'm trying to get us out—"

Beep.

Both Logan and his dad looked up when the bell sounded at the entry door.

"Expecting anyone?"

Logan shook his head.

"Who's there?" his dad's voice boomed.

"Investigation Force from One World Galaxy Foundation. Are you Mr. Kane?"

His dad's face went white. He stood, grabbing the type pad from the floor. Within two steps he was in the kitchen, shoving the device into the drawer. "Um, yeah," he yelled. "Just a minute."

"Sir, we'd like to ask you some questions. It will only take a moment. May we come in?"

Logan slunk against the wall. "Activate security screen," he whispered.

The security system responded immediately. The screen above the entry door gave a live view of four robots, heavily armed, weapons pointed at the door.

Sweat glistened on his dad's face. "If they arrest me, they'll send you straight to Juvi Hall as a co-conspirator."

The room jolted as a laser blast shot through the door.

Chapter Twenty-Six
BROKEN

His dad's arms covered him in protection.

"Dad, I can get us both out of here, but you have to trust me."

The robots burst in. "Freeze! Drop any weapons and put your hands in the air."

Logan's dad shot his arms into the air as a robot pulled Logan away from him.

"Logan, if you can get yourself out of here, do it," his dad shouted. "Now!"

Logan pressed the button on his wrist remote, hands shaking.

Then Amy's backyard fence appeared before him.

He crouched down, catching his breath, leaning his head against the white-painted wood. *Will Dad fight them? Are they going to kill him?*

"Logan?"

He lifted his head.

"Can you help me? Dumb thing is leaking gas." Amy fiddled with the grass cutter.

"I need a map. A good one, for Havilah and Pishon."

"Well, that's just lovely, because I need a working lawn mower." She kicked the machine. "Mom said I'm grounded if I don't finish cutting the grass tonight. We've got the co-op coming in the morning, and she's freaking out about our place being ready for company."

Logan grabbed her arm. "Listen to me. I need that map now."

"Let go of me." She jerked herself back. "You're not the only one with problems, you know." She bent over the lawn mower and pulled the starter rope.

Logan grabbed the mower and heaved it upside down.

"What is the matter with you?" she shouted.

"I need to get to my mom," he said through his teeth. "And that won't happen without that map for the gold."

"Why do you need a map for gold when you can just time travel yourself to wherever she is?" She grabbed at the handle bar of the mower, trying to turn it upright.

Logan blinked. "Yeah … I can just go … to Earth." He looked at his wrist remote as if seeing it anew. "Whenever I want. At whatever time period I want." A smile slowly spread over his face. "Amy, you're brilliant!"

"It's about time you figured that out."

He didn't waste a second punching information into his wrist remote. Where was his mom again? He stopped and lifted his head. "Amy?"

She sat on the edge of the mower, looking dejected, hands cupping her chin.

"I can't remember the name of the city. It's something like Denveer ... or Dunvar ... in Colorado." He let out a frustrated sigh.

"Denver, Colorado."

"She's at the Global Recovery Science Center. Does that sound familiar? Do you know which part of Denver that would be in?"

"Never heard of it." She got up and walked away.

"Where are you going?"

"I have to get this lawn mown, and talking to you isn't getting me anywhere. I'm gonna find Ben and see if he can help me fix it."

"Wait. Help me out with this, and I'll help you get the lawn mown."

Taking a deep breath, she turned. "All right. Just make it quick. I have to finish by sundown." She walked to him. "What do you need?"

"Come with me. Help me find the station. I can't waste time like I did trying to find the gold."

"No way. I am *not* doing time travel again. I almost got eaten by a T-Rex."

"But I'm completely lost on Earth. You've been there before."

"You mean I *am* here."

"I'm going to help you get the grass cut. Remember?"

She blew out an exasperated breath. "Fine. Let's go." She took hold of his arm, and the grassy yard disappeared.

They stood in the middle of a street. Or what used to be a street. Ash-covered chunks of pavement and rubble lay in piles. A few tall buildings still stood with broken windows. Cars parked on the side of the road had flat tires or were completely smashed from fallen debris.

The silence felt eerie.

Amy spun. "Denver did not look like this when we visited. What year is this?"

"Twenty thirty-six."

She climbed a rubble heap and looked around. "What happened?"

"Earthquakes. Volcanoes." His voice sounded hollow. "All over the world." *How could Mom have survived?*

"Whoa. Is that why you're living on the moon?"

COSMIC CHAOS

He nodded. "Let's go. I need to find my mom."

A broken street sign above them dangled from its post, moving with the slight breeze.

Movement down the street caught Logan's eye.

A pack of wild dogs. Headed straight for them.

"Amy." Logan backed up, watching the animals with their heads low and snarling, coming fast.

"If there was a science center before, there's nothing here now."

"Amy, run!" Logan pulled at her arm and ran to a building's door. He pulled at the door, but it was locked.

They scrambled over a high pile of debris and discovered an area barely affected by the quakes. The flat road made for faster running.

He grabbed at the next building's door and swung it open, shoving her in.

Snarling teeth lunged at Logan. He held his arm up to block the dog from snapping at his face, knocking the animal down. Another dog jumped at him, catching the wrist remote in his teeth, ripping it off Logan.

He dove inside while Amy pulled the door closed.

Through the glass doors they watched as the dog crushed the remote in his jaws.

"The remote," Amy shrieked.

The dog chewed for a bit, then dropped the pieces

before he rejoined the other dogs in barking and snarling at the door.

"It's broken!" Amy went hysterical. "We're stuck here forever. I'm stuck in the future." She punched Logan's chest repeatedly. "Don't just stand there; do something!"

"What do you expect me to do?" Logan shouted. "Open the door and get eaten?" He walked away, farther into the large room they'd entered. A sign over the front desk said *Diamond Banking.* Overstuffed couches and brown leather chairs filled the waiting area, covered with cobwebs. A wide staircase with fancy scrolled railing went up to a balcony.

"I don't care what you do, just do *something*," she said.

He went up the stairs. Maybe this was just a nightmarish dream and not real.

At the top of the stairs, past the balcony, were several doors.

He opened the first one and crossed the room to the window.

From upstairs, he had a better view of the city.

It looked so barren, broken, and lost.

Just like me. Somehow he needed to get the wrist remote without becoming dog chow.

Maybe the dogs will leave. Then I can get the remote. But if

172

it's broken, how am I going to fix it?

His insides twisted. *Hopeless.*

On the wall, a massive one-hundred-dollar bill was framed, its green paper faded. *In God We Trust.*

When Amy broke her ankle, she prayed.

And God answered.

Would that work for me?

"God?" He looked behind him, making sure Amy wasn't there to hear him. "If you're really out there ..." His throat tightened. "I ... I need help." He squeezed his eyes closed. "Please, help me." He waited, then slowly opened his eyes to look around.

Everything seemed the same.

No warrior angel to fight off the dogs, no waking up from a nightmare.

Nothing.

He stared down at the floor. How stupid to think that God would help him.

Amy. An urgency filled his mind to go to her. *Now.*

But she was probably still freaking out. He didn't need her screaming at him.

An overwhelming sense came again that he needed to go downstairs.

Maybe she's scared. And I should probably go apologize to her. He blew out a sigh and sat on a nearby swivel chair. He just didn't have it inside him to deal with her right now.

And then, like a roll of the sea, the urgent need to go to her swept over him.

Finally, he stood and rushed to the balcony. He saw her and gasped.

Below him, she stood on a chair, leaning out a broken window at one side of the main lobby. She tossed out the contents of a bag to the sidewalk. "Here doggie, doggie!"

The snarling animals left the front door, ran along the wall of windows, and rushed at the food, fighting, growling, and snapping at the packaged food she'd dropped.

Amy leaped from the chair and ran to the entrance. With the coast clear, she opened the door and grabbed the wrist remote as well as the small broken pieces, then rushed back inside.

Logan trotted down the staircase. "Whoa! I thought you'd be down here crying, and here you are saving the world. Where did you find all that food?"

She pointed. "There's an employee lounge in—"

A light on the wrist remote began to blink.

Amy looked at Logan, eyes widening.

He dove from the last step of the staircase to where she stood, grabbing her arm, watching with horror as she began to disappear before him.

Chapter Twenty-Seven
ABANDONED

Logan and Amy appeared in a crumpled heap, just outside the toolshed.

Ben stood there with a guilty look on his face. "I'm sorry! I didn't mean to do it."

Amy pulled herself up from the ground, rubbing a sore shoulder. "Ben," she grabbed him and hugged him tight. "I thought I'd never see you again." She let out a breath. With her arms still around Ben, she turned. "We made it, Logan." She laughed. "We're back!"

Amy was home! His prayer had been answered.

Maybe God is real. Maybe. But what about me? With the wrist remote broken, how can I get home? What about Dad?

Ben pulled away. "Can you make me a peanut-butter-and-jelly sandwich now?"

Amy looked at him funny. "What are you talking about?"

"I was in my room and needed a sandwich really, really bad. I couldn't find you anywhere."

"And?"

"I went in the toolshed and asked the bionic woman."

Logan stiffened. "You were not supposed to touch her again!"

Amy held up her hand. "Let him finish. Then what happened, Ben?"

He gave a wary look at Logan before answering. "I kept hearing a voice in my head to get her to wake up. It was so weird."

A sense of knowing washed over Logan. His prayer. This is how God had answered his prayer.

"I pushed on her buttons. I really wanted someone to make me that sandwich."

"I can help you," a voice said. Nanny stood at the open shed door. Fully awake. She gave Logan a calculated stare. "You left me."

Logan swallowed hard and backed up.

She stepped forward, still staring. "I'm assigned to care for you. Yet you abandoned me."

"Did you bring us back just now?" Amy asked.

Nanny continued to stare at Logan. "No. One of the buttons Ben pressed activated the wrist remote."

Amy held up the wrist remote. "This is broken. Can you fix it?"

Nanny took the wrist remote and examined it. "Yes." She scanned it with laser eyes.

COSMIC CHAOS

A drill popped from her finger.

She used it to open the remote, repair it, and close it again.

Amy cleared her throat. "Logan has to get to the Global Recovery Science Center in Denver, in the year twenty thirty-six. Can you help him?"

Logan lifted his hands to caution her. If Amy mentioned his mom, Nanny would probably break his neck right there. He took a few steps back, wishing he could disappear.

"Yes," Nanny answered in a monotone voice.

Logan's jaw dropped. Maybe Nanny was nicer in the presence of other people.

The robot handed the remote to Logan, drilling him with her eyes. She pushed some buttons on her open panel. "I've set your coordinates to the Global Recovery Science Center in Denver, Colorado. There's a security lock over the area that I can't penetrate. But I can at least put you near the compound."

Maybe Ben reset her or something with all that button-pushing. Maybe she didn't remember being angry. *How did I get so lucky?*

"You are set to go, Logan." Nanny put a hand on Ben's small shoulder. "Ben will stay with me until you return."

Ben tilted his head to look up at her. "You're gonna

177

make me a sandwich?"

"Yes," Nanny said, a sinister smile curving up the side of her mouth. "Show me where to find the kitchen."

"Wait a minute," Logan said. "I don't like this."

Nanny turned to face him. "You have no choice, Logan. If you don't return to me, Ben will face the consequences." She clutched the little boy's wrist and squeezed.

"Ow!" Ben cried out. "Let go of me."

Logan felt numb with shock. He looked at Ben, then at Amy.

"What's she talking about?" Amy asked. "What's she doing?"

Nanny pushed a button on the still-open panel. "You have two hours within the program before you must return to me."

"Wait, this isn't going to work, you can't—"

Ben screamed.

The wrist remote blinked, taking Logan back to Denver. A huge building loomed in front of him.

Global Recovery Science Center.

His breathing quickened.

Mom was in there. Somewhere.

He swallowed hard. His footsteps felt heavy. *But what about Ben? What kind of consequences was Nanny talking about?* He had a sinking feeling he already knew the answer.

He came to the doors, but they wouldn't slide open.

A security scanner stood in a short pillar at the edge of the right door.

Without a badge, he couldn't enter. Which meant he'd have to wait until someone went in and he could follow. But how much time was that going to eat up?

He tucked himself into some bushes nearby. *I'll follow someone in, hurry and find Mom, then time travel with her to Amy's house.*

A man walked by, a security badge on a lanyard around his neck. He stopped at the scanner to wave the badge.

The doors immediately slid open.

Logan hurried in behind him. On camera, it might appear they were together.

The man continued through the lobby.

Logan crouched behind a large, potted plant and scanned the area.

Two robots manned the main counter, working at computers. Above their heads, on the wall, was a directory.

Which floor would his mom be on?

Volcanology and Seismology – 4th floor

He looked at the elevators. He'd have to get over

179

there without being seen. He looked both ways to make sure the coast was clear, then made a run for it.

"Halt!" A security robot zoomed through the air toward him, powered by jet packs, gun aimed right at Logan.

Logan stopped, raising his hands in the air.

Chapter Twenty-Eight
SECURITY

"Show your security pass," the guard said.

"I don't have one. My mom is a scientist here and I—"

"Silence. This is a secure facility. No one is allowed to enter without authorization." He clipped handcuffs over Logan's wrists and pulled him along.

He tried to discreetly push a button, any button, on his wrist remote, but couldn't quite do it with his hands cuffed. Logan jerked and pulled. "Let go."

The robots at the desk were watching.

He pleaded for their help. "My mom is a scientist here. I need to see her. It's an emergency!"

They stared at him with unfeeling eyes.

The security guard pulled him into a stairwell, going down.

"Where are you taking me?"

"That's classified."

Finally, they reached a door with a sign titled *Galaxy Water Transport*.

Inside, the room buzzed in activity. A variety of robots worked to prepare a massive transportation pod. It stood on rails in the middle of the room. On its side, in big blue letters, was *GWT*.

The security guard shoved Logan forward to the main desk. "I'm sending this kid to Venus. He needs to ride in your water pod to connect with the prison transport on the moon."

The desk robot spoke into an intercom that blasted through the entire room. "Carl." Her voice echoed through the warehouse. "You've got a passenger for your route today."

Hundreds of gallons of water poured into the pod from tubes above.

As soon as the tubes ran dry, the security guard pushed Logan forward. "Get inside."

Logan sat down in the passenger seat.

The cab had a sleek, smooth interior. Everything looked clean and well-maintained. Which meant nothing sticking out to pry the cuffs off with.

Carl eased into the seat next to him with a flashy, silver grin. "It's been a long time since I've had someone ride with me."

Carl's face seemed so real—the sparkling eyes, the dimple in the cheeks, the way he formed words with such articulation—except his entire face was made of shimmering silver. The rest of his body seemed more bulky, built for hauling water coolers, but still gleamed the same way.

Carl settled behind the controls.

"Listen, Carl, I'm not a bad person. I just need to find my mom."

Carl pressed his metal finger into the ignition, and the pod fired up.

"Please. Let me go. My mom is here. I'm so close!"

Carl stared ahead. "I have to follow orders. Sorry, kid."

They zoomed forward at an excessive speed. Two massive doors opened to the outside. The pod propelled even faster, and the incline got so steep Logan's breath caught in his throat. Finally, the pod left the rails and shot into the sky, at warp speed, plastering Logan to the back of the seat. Blue sky flew by, then they entered the blackness of space. Without slowing, they headed straight for the moon.

Finally, the pressure eased up.

The earth became smaller and smaller behind them. Vibrant blues and green. Swirls of white clouds.

"Whoa." Logan couldn't hold it in. "The earth looks amazing."

Carl nodded. "Yes, the earth has stabilized. The volcanoes are sleeping, tsunamis are no longer an issue, and as you can see, the volcanic ash that permeated the air has settled." He moved forward to adjust the pressure in the cabin. "No other land masses have collapsed into the oceans since the catastrophe, so the mud has settled to the bottom of the seas."

That made no sense. Why hadn't his mom come to get him? And ... "Then why does it still look so bad from the moon?"

Carl looked at him with an amused expression. "The image you see from the moon is a projection. You're seeing the earth as it was five years ago."

The air left Logan's lungs. "Why would they lie to us like that?"

"That, young man, is classified information. I don't even know the answer. I just haul the water."

"But I thought all water transports were stopped."

"They were. For the general public." Carl winked at him. "I'm still making deliveries for key leaders and the wealthy."

Logan shot him an exasperated look. "I suppose the key leaders and the wealthy aren't rationed with food and oxygen, either."

Carl nodded. "You're correct."

"That's not right."

"Just doing my job." Carl swiveled at the waist, turning toward Logan. "Have you ever had real water before?"

Logan hesitated. If he told the truth, he'd have to explain about the time travel.

"Today I'm carrying melted snow from the Rocky Mountains. Good stuff. At least that's what humans tell me."

Carl watched Logan for a moment, as if considering something. "I've got some samples over there. Tropical rain water, high mountain water, melted icebergs. Only the very best of the best." He motioned with his head. "They're right behind my seat. Grab one."

Logan lifted his hands to show Carl his restraints.

Carl reached over and pressed a button on the cuffs. "That should loosen them up enough." He gave a stern eye. "Just don't try anything. I'm a trained kung fu master."

Logan laughed. Hopefully what he was about to do wouldn't get Carl into trouble.

"Trust me, once you taste this, you'll never be satisfied with synthetic water again."

Logan stood up and reached behind the seat. He chose a water sample titled *Mountain Gorge Springs*. He peeled the lid off the little cup and drank down the clear, cool, refreshing liquid.

Not as good as the water in Eden, but much better than synthetic water.

"This is amazing."

Carl's teeth shimmered as his smile grew. "Try another. Each kind has a distinct flavor."

Logan pretended to grab for one more, but instead, he pushed the button on his wrist remote to backtrack.

Within a millisecond, he found himself at the front of the science center. Only this time he was wearing cuffs.

Great. He held them up. What could he accomplish with these on?

Someone stood with their back to Logan, right in front of him! He dove behind a pillar and watched as the person hid behind the bushes.

Wait. That's me!

Crossing his own time stream, he waited for his first self to go inside, then he followed. Instead of heading toward the main lobby, Logan went to the staircase. He ran as fast as he could up the stairs to the Volcanology and Seismology room on the fourth floor.

He ducked inside the door and crouched low next to a counter.

Tagged samples of volcanic rock and ash lined the walls on the shelves. The counters were filled with bottles, telescopes, and chart notes. A large map of the world was displayed on one wall, flags marking different volcanoes.

COSMIC CHAOS

He peeked around the corner. Several scientists in lab coats stood at large machines, discussing test results with other scientists, who sat in front of a myriad of computers.

One of the women responded to something someone else said, her voice strong and clear.

Mom.

He felt detached, as if in a dream. He watched her talk, her mouth in an easy smile. Her eyes seemed warm and caring, but there was something there not quite as obvious. A sadness.

He watched her with fascination, taking in everything about her from a distance. She wore her brown hair swept up in a loose bun, some strands resting at her cheeks. She concentrated on the sample in front of her, examining it under a microscope. He wanted to approach her, but realized it would be safer when no one else was around. He looked around the room, hoping to find a better place to hide.

The door opened behind him.

He scrambled deeper into the samples.

"There you are," the security guard said. "I saw you come in on the security footage." He grabbed Logan by the elbow.

"Wait, no!" Trying to pull his arm free, he turned and screamed, "Mom!"

Scientists came running forward, staring at Logan.

As the guard tightened the cuffs, Logan looked at his mom with pleading eyes. "Mom, don't you recognize me?"

She put her hands to her face. "Logan," she said in whispered awe. She ran to him, all the scientists parting to make way for her.

The guard yanked on Logan's elbow, pulling him to the door.

"Wait," she said with authority. "This is"—her voice quavered—"my son."

"Mrs. Kane," the guard said, "he can't stay here. You know the rules."

Logan jerked out of the guard's grip and threw himself into his mother's arms. He pressed into her warmth and scent and the rhythm of her heart beating, not wanting to leave her. Ever.

Her tears spilled onto his fuzzy head, then she pulled him back at arm's length. "Let me look at you." She wiped at her eyes as she examined him from head to toe. "My, how you've grown. Oh, I've missed you so much." She pulled him into another hug. "Where's Paul?"

"Who?"

COSMIC CHAOS

His mom's smile dropped as she examined his face. "Paul. Your father."

"Oh." Logan looked around at the other scientists, all staring at him.

She looked at him in an odd way. Then she turned her attention to the security guard. "He'll be staying with me."

"He's not authorized to be in the compound."

She stood her ground. "I'm authorizing him with code eighty-four."

The guard stiffened. "Yes, ma'am." He stepped forward and removed Logan's handcuffs.

One of the other scientists came over and patted Logan on the arm. Jerry Benson, according to his name tag. "When you're the top scientist in the compound, the guards do whatever you say." His nasally laugh filled the room.

"Come, sit down." His mom gently pulled Logan to an empty table and motioned toward a chair. "Tell me how you've been, what brought you here. Tell me everything!"

Logan had so much to share, he didn't know where to begin. And how much was safe to tell her?

She wiped at her eyes and nose with a tissue.

The other scientists resumed their work at their different stations, allowing them a bit of privacy.

They sat in awkward silence for a moment.

"Mom, why haven't you called?"

She gave an uneasy glance at the other scientists. "It's complicated. Believe me, I would be calling every day if the One World Galaxy Foundation hadn't cut off public lines of communication." She looked so sad.

"But everything looks fine here. And you promised to come get me when the earth was safe again." He swallowed hard, keeping his eyes on the table to keep tears from spilling over. "You *promised.*"

She nodded, not holding back her own tears.

"Why didn't you just keep me with you?" He put his hands over his face.

"Do you remember why you had to leave and why I stayed?" Her voice took on a soft tenderness.

Logan shook his head. He pushed the tears from his eyes with balled fists and searched her face. "I don't remember much. I was only seven."

"The seismic activity across the globe had become a huge concern years before you left. The One World Galaxy Foundation had been formed out of necessity, making extensive plans to keep mankind safe in the event of an emergency. They sent work crews to the moon to build biodomes. Do you remember watching the holographic images with me, when they sent live images to Earth showing their progress?"

"Maybe." Logan thought for a moment. "Yeah, I do remember."

She gave a soft smile, then her expression grew serious again. "But then ..." Her voice trailed off, as though she was troubled by the memory.

"But then the catastrophe hit." He finished the sentence for her.

She sighed. "Yes. One morning, it took us all by surprise. A tectonic plate shifted in the Pacific Ocean, activating volcanoes in the Ring of Fire." She pointed to the map of volcanoes on the wall. "Ash filled the air, tsunamis hit the coasts, land masses like California collapsed into the oceans. Many, many lives were lost. And Earth continued to tremble."

"And that's when we left."

She nodded. "That's when the emergency evacuations began. The moon and Venus weren't completely ready, but the Foundation didn't want to risk losing any more lives."

"I need to stay with you, Mom. I hate living on the moon. And I miss you so much."

"I've missed you too." She put her hand over his and squeezed. "The last time I talked to your father, he said you were still very sick. But looking at you now … you look fantastic. Like you just returned from a vacation in Florida. You even have hair!" She rubbed her other hand over his fuzzy scalp.

Every touch of her hands seemed to fill Logan with a sense of comfort. He gave her a lopsided smile. "Yeah, I've been feeling a lot better. But then, I haven't been on the moon much lately."

Her smile dropped into concern. "Why? Where have you been?"

"I've been here on Earth. Just during different time periods."

"You mean in interactive programs?"

"No, I mean time travel."

His mom looked stunned, then looked around nervously.

Both Jerry and another scientist looked their way.

"Hon, I think we need to talk somewhere more private." Her voice sounded wobbly as her hand tightened on his.

"Call security," Jerry spoke to another scientist. He pushed up the black-framed glasses that slid down his nose. "Now!"

Chapter Twenty-Nine
ON THE RUN

Logan's mom grabbed his hand and yanked him out of the room and down the hallway. She looked both directions before turning to him. "You're scaring me, Logan," she said quietly. "Are you certain it's time travel?"

He nodded. "Positive."

She let out a heavy sigh. "I've heard discussions here about a Nanny Express Five Thousand hiding a stolen chip. The technology exists, but it's extremely dangerous." She started walking again, at a fast pace.

More like Nanny *is extremely dangerous.* He wondered if Ben was okay. *I need to get back soon, before the two hours expire.*

"You're using the time travel chip that was stolen from the Cryo Labs on the moon?"

He nodded. "I'm pretty sure."

"We have to get you out of here. You're not safe. When Jerry reports what he heard, you'll be sent directly to prison, whether you have the chip by accident or not." Still holding his hand, she pulled him into a run. "They took you away from me when you were just seven years old. I won't let them do it again."

They rode the elevators down to the main level and sped to the rear of the building, then through the double doors and to the parking lot.

Carts were plugged in at different posts. They looked like egg-shaped golf carts, with sleek upper and side panels, extra-wide all-terrain tires, and an open compartment in the back for equipment.

"Mine's the one on the end. It's supposed to charge for another two hours before I go out again, but we don't have time."

"Where are we going?"

"Anywhere but here." She unplugged her cart and sat in the driver's seat. Logan climbed in, and they zipped down the road.

"Maybe I can take you to our old home. Would you like to see where we used to live?"

"Absolutely. Can we stay there?"

"No. There's no access to water there."

He shot her a questioning look.

"There's just no one to repair or operate those things now." She tapped at the control panel on the cart. "I don't know if this thing has enough energy to make it. We might need to walk part of the way."

They passed the security gates.

"It's too bad we couldn't just go to your grandma's farm," she said. "That place would be perfect. But it's eight hundred miles away."

"I have a grandma?"

"Yes." She looked at him. "Oh, honey, you didn't know?"

"Mom, why didn't you just come with us when we went to the moon?"

She let out a hard laugh. "I was required to stay because of my expertise in the field." She pressed a knee to the steering wheel to hold it steady while pulling off her white lab coat. "I'm managing a team that evaluates danger levels in the seismic activity as well as monitoring magnetic and gravity changes. My work determines when it's safe for everyone to return." She flung the coat into the back.

A small tool belt was wrapped around her waist. A gun, in its holster, was mounted on her upper thigh.

"If I refused to stay, I would have been imprisoned on Venus."

"That's just wrong. I still wouldn't have seen you."

"At least being here, I thought there was a chance to get you back." She reached above his knees to open a compartment and pulled out a pair of sunglasses. "But when Jerry figured out how to tap into the

Foundation's news broadcast and we heard they put the moon into lockdown, I decided to take matters into my own hands."

"What do you mean?"

"At the evacuation site, not far from here, they left two Janskys. They're mini jet-propelled rockets on standby for the scientists if an emergency escape is ever needed. I have my bag packed and ready to go. I figured if you couldn't come down, I'd go up." She smiled, lifting her eyebrows. "But you got to me first."

Something in the side mirror caught Logan's attention. In the distance a group of black, armored robots wearing jet packs, just like the guard in the lobby, flew toward them. Their weapons were drawn.

"Mom? Are those guys coming after us?"

His mom looked in the rearview mirror and gasped.

Shots fired.

"Get down!" She pressed his head below the seat top.

A tire blew, sending them careening to the side of the road, the green cart toppling on its side.

Logan tumbled out into the tall grass on the edge of the road.

His mom's pant leg was ripped, but the scrape on her leg didn't look too bad. Using the cart as a shield, she pulled the gun from her holster and pointed at the oncoming robots. The gun activated, its stock glowing with blue electrons, as if securely responding to her unique fingerprints. Power-up indicators along the fat barrel lit as if it was ready to fire.

"What is that thing?" Logan scrambled to her side. "It looks vicious."

"A stun gun. It's meant for wild animals, but it'll slow the guards down. It's all we've got."

"Mom."

She shot the stun gun on full power, releasing a wicked, blue stream of lightning.

The stream hit one of the airborne robots, causing it to flip and crash to the pavement. The other robots scattered for cover behind trees.

She watched the indicators on the gun, apparently waiting for it to power back up.

"Mom," he said, more firmly this time.

She looked down at him. "Not now." She took aim again.

"I need you to tell me Grandma's address."

She spouted off the location without looking at him. "We won't make it. It's too far." Her voice sounded frantic. "You're going to have to run."

"Put the stun gun down and hang on to me." Logan rested his hand on her arm.

She looked at him.

COSMIC CHAOS

"Just do it." He stared hard at her frightened face. "Trust me, okay?"

She put the gun in its holster and wrapped an arm around him in a hug.

With the address already entered, Logan pressed the destination button on his wrist remote.

Slowly, a farmhouse emerged in front of them.

His mom gasped. "How did you do that?" She turned all the way around, as if looking for any sign of the guards.

A two-story house stood before them. The light-blue paint was peeling, and the screen door was nearly falling off its hinges. The front porch sagged. An old pickup truck sat in the driveway, looking as if it'd been there for over fifty years.

"The house is still standing," his mom said in awe. "I haven't been here since before you were born."

A big, red barn stood behind it. A clucking sound came from nearby.

"Oh, my. The chickens are still here! Maybe a little wild, but we could domesticate them."

"We could live here?"

She hugged Logan hard. "Just wait till you see what's in the basement. Your grandma kept supplies for emergencies, like first aid kits and lots of candles. And she used to can everything she grew." His mom rubbed her chin on Logan's head as her words became quiet. "But she had to leave it all behind when everyone was shipped to the moon."

"Grandma was sent to the moon? Why haven't I ever seen her? None of my friends have grandmas, either."

"We were told that everyone over the age of sixty was sent to a private biodome, where they would receive special care. However, after all the lies the government has fed us, I have a feeling your grandma may be in trouble."

She took a deep breath and held Logan at arm's length, looking him over with a smile. "Anyway, we'll have enough food to last us until we can grow our own."

"Anything will be better than the gray mush I've been eating."

She scrunched up her nose. "Your dad told me about that. I'll make it up to you. Lots of savory, homemade food from here on out." She paused for a moment, putting her hands on her hips. "We'll have to go out to the pump behind the barn to get water, since there's no running water in the house." She winked at him. "It's going to be tough living here, but worth it." She took his hand and walked around to the back of the house. "Fruit trees. Look at that. There's fruit already growing. Peaches, apples, pears. They'll be ready and ripe later this summer." She let out a deep sigh. "We'll be just fine here, Logan. Just fine."

The distinct hum of a plasma-propelled ship sounded in the distance.

"Mom, is that coming this way?"

She jerked her head up and reached into her tool belt. "Hurry, get into the house." She turned to him. "Just be careful where you step. The house was already in need of repairs when Grandma left, and the seismic activity likely made it worse." She pulled out a device, set it down in the front yard, and pulled a lever.

A blue laser shot out of the device, up into the sky, then dropped over and around them and the house like a clear bubble.

Logan held the front door open for her as she sprinted in. "What is that thing?"

She sat near the front room's window on a dusty old couch. "An invisible force field. We use them to protect an area we're pulling samples from when the weather is bad. That ship won't be able to detect us when they scan over the house."

"What are they scanning for?"

"Robots are in those ships, searching for human life. There's only supposed to be scientists at the center. But I've heard rumors that many people have escaped from the moon and are hiding on Earth."

"I don't get it. Why don't they just let people stay on Earth?"

"Like I said before, it's complicated."

"Tell me, Mom." Logan watched her face, waiting for an answer.

She stared up, through the window, as the ship passed overhead. "I was worried you and your dad would try something like that. Escaping. Sometimes Paul has crazy ideas and I can't talk him out of them."

"Mom, Dad *was* trying to get us off the moon. He got arrested."

She sat up straighter, putting her hands over her mouth.

"But don't worry. I can time travel and bring him here before he gets arrested."

"I would love that." Her face lit up with hope. "I've missed him so much."

"Yeah, I've missed him too."

"What? What do you mean? Hasn't he been on the moon with you?"

"Yes, but ..." Logan sighed. "The oxygen systems he helped create while on Earth don't function as well on the moon. Something about atmospheric pressure. So he's at the facility twenty-four hours a day."

"He always was a hard worker. But, Logan, who's

been taking care of you?"

He lifted a shoulder, giving his head a slight shake.

"Oh, no, no, no. *Please* don't tell me you've been on your own all these years."

"Robots took care of me."

She choked back a sob. "I have failed you."

"But, Mom, we're together now. And that's what matters." He wrapped an arm around her shoulders. "I'm going to get Dad and Grandma here too. We'll be a family again."

"This whole time travel thing is scary, Logan. You need to be really careful. Especially if it gets into the wrong hands. There's a lot of evil in this galaxy."

Nanny! How much time has passed? Way more than two hours. What if Ben is already dead?

Chapter Thirty
LOST TIME

"I'm going down to the basement to do some food inventory," said his mom. "Most of it is probably spoiled by now, but there may be some jars of pickles or peaches that are still good. Hopefully, I'll find the candles and matches too. We'll need them tonight."

Considering the stress she was under, she didn't need to hear about psycho Nanny. Logan waited until her footsteps sounded on the stairs, then lifted his wrist remote and whispered, "Nanny?"

No response.

Now what do I do? Logan looked out the window.

What would Amy do? He knew the answer to that. He bowed his head. *God, if that's really You that answered my prayer before, please make it possible for me to spend more time with Mom. I don't want to go back to Nanny. But I can't just leave her there to hurt Ben. What do I do?*

A gentle knowing came over him. He should go to Amy's house.

Logan's eyes flew open. But there were so many

reasons why he shouldn't go to Amy's. *My time is already up. Nanny may have killed them all by now. She's going to kill me next. God, what do I do?*

He should go to Amy's.

There it was again. Unmistakable. Without thinking about it this time, Logan lifted his wrist remote. "Nanny?"

No response.

"Hey, Mom?" he called out. "I gotta go. There's something I need to do."

"Are you time traveling?" Her steps hurried up the creaking wooden stairs. "I'm coming with you."

"No, I can't risk anything happening to you. Please, stay here." He gave her a reassuring look. "Trust me. I'll be back as soon as I can."

"No. You are not going alone. I'm coming." Her voice had the same firm tone she'd used with the guard at the science center. She started toward him.

He shook his head, backed away, and pressed the button on his wrist remote.

The room disappeared as the scent of freshly cut grass filled his nose.

"Logan!" Amy said. She was pushing the mower into the toolshed. "You made it back. Did you find your mom?"

"Yes. And she's safe." He searched Amy's face,

looking for signs of distress. "Where are Ben and Nanny?" He examined the backyard.

The grass was perfectly cut.

"Oh, just wait till you see." She laughed "Nanny fixed the lawn mower. But I didn't even need it because she used a laser beam to cut the grass for me. She's amazing!" Amy grabbed his arm. "And there's more."

Inside, Nanny worked in the kitchen. Her hands flew at lightning speed, washing pots and pans.

"Nanny?" Logan asked.

Nanny turned her head toward Logan while her hands continued to wash in a frenzy. A huge grin plastered her face, and some sort of glitch caused her head to jerk back and forth a little.

Logan stepped back in alarm. He turned to Amy. "What happened?"

"She was getting really nasty and hurting Ben. You wouldn't believe the bruise she put on his arm."

Logan rubbed his own shoulder where Nanny had hurt him in the same way.

"No way was I gonna let her hurt my little brother and get away with it. She was messin' with the wrong family."

"What did you do?"

"I grabbed the hoe from the toolshed and gave her a good whack in the head."

"You what?"

"Sorry, Logan. I know Nanny is the time machine, but you should have heard Ben screaming. I couldn't take it anymore."

"And then?"

"While she was out cold, Ben played around with her circuit board. He did all sorts of rewiring."

Ben walked into the kitchen. "Logan, you're here!"

"Yeah." Logan looked down at Ben.

The purplish bruise on his wrist was hard to miss.

"So what exactly did you do to Nanny?"

"You know that little, red chip that was inside her? I think it was blocking her safety components, and that's why she was being so mean. I adjusted some of her circuits that weren't as important to make room for the red chip. That's why her head jerks around so much. Wanna see what I did?"

"No, no. I believe you." A wave of gratitude welled up inside him. This kid wasn't a waste of his time after all. "You did good, Ben. Really good."

"Anyway," Amy said, "she seems to be working great."

Logan stared at Nanny. It couldn't be that easy.

"I explained to my parents that she's a robot, and I showed them the panel Ben discovered. They were astounded." A smile spread across her face. "I told them I offered to take care of Nanny for a while, until you return, 'cause you and your mom are scientists, doing super important work."

"And they were okay with that?"

"They were skeptical at first, but I reminded my mom that she met you already when you borrowed her Bible. And then when they saw how helpful Nanny is, they agreed."

"So everything's fine." If he could leave Nanny with Amy's family, it would make it less awkward. He could only imagine trying to get to know Mom with Nanny always there, hearing every word. "Amy, can she stay here longer?"

Ben piped up from behind him. "Yes. I showed her a cookbook and asked her to make cookies. And she made every cookie recipe I asked for."

Logan laughed. "Really?"

Ben nodded. "We ended up freezing all that cookie dough, or we'd have enough to feed the planet."

"We'd love it if she stayed here," Amy said. "With Nanny doing all the chores, Mom might be able to get that degree she's always wanted."

A lightness filled Logan's heart. *God answered my prayer. Again.* "Well, Amy," he said, in awe, "since you guys are getting along so well with her, I'm going back to my mom. Have Nanny contact me if you need anything. I'll be wearing the wrist remote."

Amy nodded. "When will you be back?"

"I'm not sure." He looked at the floor, not knowing how to answer her. "Amy … thanks … for all your help. For everything." He gave her an awkward handshake.

Ben lifted his hand for a high-five. "Want a peanut-butter-and-jelly sandwich to take with you?"

Logan smiled, smacking his hand against Ben's. "Yeah, buddy. I'll take two."

Nanny immediately set to work, creating two sandwiches and bagging them.

Ben looked like a proud parent as she handed them to Logan.

"'Bye, guys," Logan said, with a catch in his throat. Saying those words felt like a meteor shower hitting his heart. He was going to miss them.

He pressed the button on his wrist remote, eager to return to the farm.

The farmhouse living room appeared. Dishes rattled and clanged in the kitchen.

He walked in to where his mom was pulling plates and glasses from the cupboards.

"There you are!" she said. "Logan Paul Kane, don't you ever disobey me like that again." A fire of fear burned in her eyes.

"Mom, I'm so sorry. Please forgive me."

"I guess you're too old to be put into time-out." A wistful smile covered her face. "The only thing I've been able to think about since they took you away from me is that I would do anything—" Her voice caught, and tears filled her eyes. "*Anything*, to be with you. I love you so much, Logan. I'm so thankful you found me, and no matter what happens, everything will be okay, because we're together again. I want us to stay together. Can you understand that?"

He did the only thing he could think of. The only thing he'd wanted to do since he first saw her. He bear-hugged her. For a good, long time.

"So you've taken care of everything, then?" she asked.

"Not everything. I still need to get Dad and Grandma."

She cradled his face with her hands. "We'll be a family again."

"Mom." He put his hands over hers, looking her squarely in the eyes. "Tell me." He used a firm, but gentle voice. "Tell me why people can't come back to Earth. Why won't the One World Galaxy Foundation allow it?"

She dropped her arms to her sides and paced the room. "Two years ago we requested the Foundation to send teams of work crews to focus on habitable areas. To clean up the rubble, restore water and sewer systems, and rebuild. But political problems arose. Instead of returning as one people, officials want countries combined and new governments established." Her voice grew agitated. "But no one is willing to give up their power. So they're at a standstill. The Foundation has become paranoid about the public finding out. All contact has been cut off from us, so we can't tell anyone up there what it's like down here. And that's why you see a different Earth being projected. They don't want to risk a riot. But people need to come home."

"I want to do that. Help people get home." Logan's sense of purpose tugged at his insides. "We have to hurry. A friend of mine changed the placement of the time travel chip inside Nanny. It's made Nanny safer for now, but I don't know how much longer the wrist remote will work. And if the Foundation finds out I've got the chip, they'll take it back."

"Okay, where do you want to go first?"

"Dad. We get Dad, then find Grandma."

"Yes, and we need to disengage the false projection of Earth. That will get everyone's attention. Then they'll be coming back in droves on their own."

"I want to make sure my friends make it here safely

too."

She nodded. "Oh, I can't wait to see your dad." She gave a nervous laugh. "I should check my hair."

"Mom, you look great. Ready?"

She nodded, barely containing her laughter.

He set the coordinates to just after his dad arrived at the apartment. "Just a warning—we'll be crossing a time stream, so there'll be two of me at my place. Be sure to stay with me and not the other Logan."

"We should have a code word, just in case I get the two of you mixed up."

"Time-out?"

She busted out laughing.

He couldn't hold it in, either. It was so good to laugh. To be near her. To soak in the truest and most wholesome joy. "I can't wait to see the look on Dad's face when he sees you."

She looped her arm through his.

Logan activated the wrist remote and the room faded.

His dad slowly came into view ...

ABOUT THE AUTHOR

Carole Marie Shelton is a wannabe time traveler and adventurer. She weaves suspense and action into her children's stories while exploring the longings of the heart (psst... she also sneaks in favorite topics like chocolate, Creation, ancient history, and dinosaurs). She squeezes in writing time between work hours and caring for her four children, ages 7 to 16. They live in a charming historic town in Oregon, where they go on hiking escapades, read books, and dream about the places they'd like to travel to someday. Learn more at www.carolemarie.com

ACKNOWLEDGMENTS

A very special thank-you ...

To my mom, for the weekend writing retreats you provided which made a huge difference in making this novel a reality.

To my kids, for your patience while I stayed in my "writing zone" for hours at a time.

To my daughter Kylie, for your valuable and brilliant input on all things sci-fi.

To my daughter Joley, for your beautiful and creative ink illustrations within this novel.

To my cousin Joey, for inspiring me to begin writing this story.

To my critique groups, especially Geneva, Cheri, Amy, and SK for your ongoing feedback, suggestions and push to keep going.

To Caleb and Brittney Breakey, for your valuable insight and encouragement.

To Drew Knox, for your honest critique from a middle grade perspective.

To my publisher, Ashberry Lane, who made my dream of becoming a published book author a reality; and my editors, who invested much time and talent into strengthening and polishing my manuscript.

And a heartfelt thank-you to every person that encouraged me to keep writing, even when life was in chaos.

Other books from Ashberry Lane

CPSIA information can be obtained
at www.ICGtesting.com
Printed in the USA
FSOW01n0433261015
12533FS